PRINCE OF
FOXES

H. L. Macfarlane

D1514024

COPYRIGHT INFORMATION

DEDICATION

For Scotland, and for faeries.

FÔX SLEEP

When someone has wakened to what is really there
is that person free of the chain of consequences
and I answered yes and with that I turned into a fox
and I have been a fox for five hundred lives
Fox Sleep (W. S. Merwin; 1992)

1

PRØLØGUE

Names were important. They always had been, from the moment man first developed language to understand the world around him. They were important, but the intense popularity of a particular playwright's work in the South of England suggested otherwise. When hoards of Londoners leeched into Scotland in search of good hunting grounds, golfing estates and other leisurely pursuits that they could not find at home Sorcha became unwillingly familiar with Shakespeare's plays.

But Sorcha and her family knew better than to take his words to heart. A rose by any other name would *not* smell as sweet, for once it lost its name it was no longer a rose as one knew it. And names weren't important simply for their superficial usage in eliminating the need to wordlessly point at things.

All her life Sorcha had the rules of names drilled into her. Do not call a person by their first name if you are not familiar with them. Take your husband's surname when you marry and leave your own behind. Bear a son to pass on his father's name. Give your children names full of luck, strength, wisdom and beauty, for they would need such traits when they grew up.

But these mantras all paled in comparison to the one rule the infuriating English tourists liked to laugh at most. They would not laugh so loudly if they knew the truth. Nobody who knew the truth laughed about it. This rule was the very reason Sorcha often went by Clara, an anglicised version of her first name that she despised but eagerly used nonetheless.

She had witnessed first-hand, as a child, what happened when you did not follow this one, most important rule. You disappeared – sometimes forever, sometimes for no time at all – but if you returned you were changed, and almost never in a good way. Sorcha had seen calm and even-tempered folk go mad, and the loudest, brashest of her father's friends retreat into their own minds, never to speak another word.

Tourists often thought the locals were crazy when they came to visit the little town of Darach. It was nestled between large, sweeping forests and breathtakingly beautiful lochs, so it was a popular place to visit away from the hustle and bustle of Glasgow and Edinburgh. Locals warned them against conversing with anyone they might meet roaming beneath the trees, or wandering along the shores of the lochs, especially at twilight. The tourists, without fail, never heeded their advice.

So they disappeared, in one fashion or another, and they only had themselves to blame. They had been warned, after all, and they didn't listen.

Never, ever give your real name to a faerie.

CHAPTER ONE

Lachlan .

Today was the queen's funeral and Lachlan, her only child and heir to the throne, was deliberately avoiding the ceremony.

His mother would understand, he was sure. He'd never been one for mournful occasions; most of the Seelie folk weren't. Their lives were long enough to be considered immortal by the humans who largely lived, unknowing and unseeing, beside them. If Lachlan allowed himself to be truly sad he'd spend centuries feeling that way.

It was the last thing he wanted.

So Lachlan was currently whiling away his morning following a human girl who was collecting early autumn brambles on the outskirts of the forest. She lived in Darach, the closest human settlement to the central realm of the Scots fair folk. The people who lived there were, in general, respectful and wary of Lachlan and his kind. They saw what members of the Seelie Court could do fairly regularly, after all. The rest of the British Isles was another story entirely, though it hadn't always been that way.

Everybody in the forest knew things were changing.

The advancements made in human medicine, and human technology, and human ingenuity, meant that humans were beginning to forget what it felt like to fear 'otherness'. They believed themselves above tales of faeries, and magic in general, though Lachlan knew there were humans capable of magic, too.

Not here, though, he thought, creeping from one tall bow of an oak tree to another to trail silently after the girl. She was happily eating one bramble for every two she placed in her basket, seemingly without a care in the world. *Not on this island. Not for centuries.* Lachlan knew this was largely because his mother, Queen Evanna – as well as King Eirian of the Unseelie Court far down south, in England – spirited all such magically-inclined British children away to the faerie realm, to live for all intents and purposes as faeries themselves.

That's certainly better than being an ordinary human, especially now, when they've forgotten about us.

A stiff breeze tearing through the oak tree caused Lachlan's solitary earring to jingle like a bell. Adorned with delicate chains and tiny sapphires, and spanning the entire length of his long, pointed ear as a cuff of beaten silver, the beautiful piece of jewellery had been a gift from his mother from a time long since passed. Back then Lachlan had been enamoured with the blue-eyed faerie, Ailith, and had been convinced the two of them would marry. The earring was ultimately meant as a gift for Ailith, he'd decided. His mother would never be so direct as to give it to Lachlan's beloved herself. It wasn't in her nature.

But then Queen Evanna had married the half-Unseelie faerie, Innis, who was the Unseelie king's brother. He had himself a grown son, Fergus, who came with his father to live in the Seelie realm. The two were silver where Lachlan and his mother were gold, and Ailith had become betrothed to his new-found stepbrother instead of him.

So Lachlan lost his love and, now, he'd lost his mother. The earring was all he had left of both.

I should go to the funeral, he decided, turning from the girl as he did so. *I am to be king, after all. I should –*

Lachlan paused. He could hear something. More chime-like than his earring in the wind, and clearer than the sound of the nearby stream flowing over centuries-smooth stone.

The human girl was singing.

"The winds were laid, the air was still,

The stars they shot alang the sky;

The fox was howling on the hill,

And the distant echoing glens reply."

Lachlan was enamoured with the sound of her voice. The words were Burns; the melody unfamiliar. He thought perhaps she'd invented the tune herself and, if so, she was a talented girl indeed. He peered through the yellowing leaves of the oak tree, intent on seeing what the human with the lovely voice truly looked like.

She was not so much a girl as a young woman – perhaps not quite twenty – though since Lachlan himself had lived for almost five times that long she was, for all intents and purposes, still simply a girl. Her skin was pale and lightly freckled, though her cheeks held onto some colour from the fast-fading summer. Her hair was a little darker than the oak trunk Lachlan was currently leaning against. It flashed like deep copper when it caught the sunlight and hung long and wild down her back, which was a sight rarely seen on a young, human woman.

A cream dress fell to her ankles and sat low on her shoulders. Small leather boots, made for wandering through forests and across meadows, were laced across her feet. A cloak of pine-coloured fabric was slung over the handle of her almost-full wicker basket. *Well-made clothes*, he concluded, *but nothing elaborate or expensive. Just an ordinary girl.* She dithered over the correct words of the next verse of her Burns poem as Lachlan merrily watched on. *Fair to look at, for a human. But it is her voice that is special. Special enough to ask her name.*

He delighted over thinking how his stepfather and stepbrother would react when he brought back a human girl, enchanted to sing for him until the end of time. *I wonder what Ailith would think. Would she be jealous? Would she mourn for the loss of my attention?*

Lachlan was excited to find out.

He stretched his arms above his head, causing his earring to jingle once more. Below him the girl stilled. She stopped singing, dark brows knitted together in confusion.

"Is somebody there?" she asked, carefully placing her basket down by her feet as she spoke.

"You have a lovely voice," Lachlan announced. He was satisfied to see the girl jump in fright, eyes swinging wildly around before she realised the voice she'd heard came from above. When she spied Lachlan standing high up on the boughs of the oak tree she gasped.

"You are – it is early to see one of your kind so far out of the forest," she said. She struggled to maintain a blank face, to appear as if she wasn't surprised in the slightest to see a faerie standing in a tree.

Lachlan laughed. "I suppose it is. Today is a special occasion; we are all very much wide awake."

The girl seemed to hesitate before responding. Lachlan figured she was trying to decide if it was wise to continue such a conversation with him. "What occasion would be so special to have you all awake before noon?"

"The funeral of the queen. My mother."

"Oh."

That was all she said. Lachan had to wonder what kind of reaction he'd expected. Certainly not sympathy; he had no use for such a thing.

"You are not at the funeral?" the girl asked after a moment of silence. "If you are her son –"

"I shall get there eventually," Lachlan replied. He sat down upon the branch he'd been standing on. "Tell me your name, lass. Your voice is too beautiful to not have a name attached to it."

To his surprise, she smiled. "I do not think so, Prince of Faeries."

Clever girl.

"You wound me," he said, holding a hand over his heart in mock dismay. "An admirer asks only for a name and you will not oblige his lowly request? How cruel you are."

"How about a name for a name, then?" she

suggested. "That seems fair."

Lachlan nodded in agreement. The girl could do nothing with his name. She was only human.

"Lachlan," he replied, with a flourish of his hand in place of a bow. "And you?"

"Clara."

"A pretty name for a pretty girl. Is there a family name to go with –"

"I am not so much a fool as to give you my family name," Clara said, "and I think you know that."

He found himself grinning. "Maybe so. Come closer, Clara. You stand so far away."

He was somewhat surprised when she boldly took a step forwards, half expecting her to decide enough was enough and run away.

Even careful humans give in to the allure of faeries, he thought, altogether rather smug. *It won't be long until I have Clara's full name.*

When Clara took another step towards him Lachlan noticed that her eyes were green.

No, blue, he decided. *No, they're –*

"Your eyes," he said, deftly swinging backwards until he was hanging upside down from the branch. Lachlan's face was now level with Clara's, though the wrong way round. She took a shocked half-step backwards at their new-found proximity. "They are strange."

"I do not think my eyes are as strange as yours, Lachlan of the forest," she replied. "Yours are gold."

"Not so uncommon a colour for a Seelie around these parts. Yours, on the other hand...we do not see mismatched eyes often."

Clara shrugged. "One blue, one green. They are not so odd. Most folk hardly notice a difference unless they stand close to me."

"Do many human boys get as close to you as I am now?" Lachlan asked, a smile playing across his lips at the blush that crossed Clara's cheeks.

She looked away. "I cannot say they have."

"Finish your song for me, Clara. I'll give you something in return."

"And what would that be?" she asked, glancing back at Lachlan. Her suspicion over the sudden change of subject was written plainly on her face.

He swung himself forwards just a little until their lips were almost touching. "A kiss, of course."

"That's...and what if I do not want that?"

"Then I guess I leave with a broken heart."

Clara's eyebrow quirked.

"You do not believe me," he complained.

"With good reason."

"You really are a cruel girl."

The two stared at each other for a while, though Lachlan was beginning to grow dizzy from his upside down view. But just as he was about to right himself, Clara took a deep breath and began to sing once more.

There were four verses left of her Burns poem, about a ghost who appeared in front of the poet to lament over what happened to him in the final years of his life, and it was both haunting and splendid to hear. Lachlan mourned for the spirit as if it had been real, and wished there was more to the poem for Clara to sing.

But eventually she sang her last, keening note, leaving only the sound of the wind to break their silence. When Lachlan crept a hand behind her neck and urged her lips to his Clara fluttered her eyes closed. The kiss was soft and chaste - hardly a kiss at all - but just as it ended Lachlan bit her lip.

The promise of something more, if Clara wanted it.

The girl was breathless and rosy-cheeked when Lachlan pulled away. A rush ran through him at the sight of her.

"Tell me your last name," he breathed, the order barely audible over the breeze ruffling Clara's hair around her face.

She opened her eyes, parting her lips as if to speak and -

The sound of bells clamoured through the air.

Clara took a step away from Lachlan immediately, eyes bright and wide and entirely lucid once more.

"I have to go," she said, stumbling backwards to pick up her forgotten basket and cloak before darting away from the forest.

No matter, Lachlan thought, as he dropped from the branch to the forest floor. *I shall see her again. I will have her name next time.*

But he was disappointed.

Now he had to go to his mother's funeral alone, with no entertainment to distract him from his grief when evening came.

CHAPTER TWO

Sorcha

"Have I lost my senses entirely?" Sorcha cried. "Singing for a faerie. Their *prince*! I must have gone mad!"

She passed Old Man MacPherson's farm in a haze of scurried footsteps, dropping brambles from the basket clutched to her chest as she went. The man's son was up on the roof; he waved to Sorcha when he noticed her, and she nodded in response. He was replacing a slate tile which had come loose and smashed upon the ground in the middle of the night. Soon the mild weather would turn and the farm would need to be as watertight as possible to avoid the coming rain, which arrived hand-in-hand with the darkest months of the year.

But Sorcha was happy with the promise of wet, cold days and wetter, colder nights. For though the creeping autumn weather and the inevitable winter that followed caused damage to roofs and fields and sometimes livestock, it also signalled a blessed end to the slew of tourists that had bombarded the tiny town of Darach since April.

Good riddance to them, Sorcha thought with vicious pleasure. *Let them return to their cities and their pollution.*

She paused by the loch-side to pick up a pair of empty glass bottles and a filthy handkerchief. Sorcha scowled; only a city-dweller would leave behind such a mess on the shore of the most beautiful loch in the country.

I'm biased, of course, she thought. *All lochs are beautiful. But Loch Lomond is...special.*

Sorcha skipped a stone across the water's surface, watching as it leapt once, twice, three times. On its fourth skip it fell beneath the dark, shimmering surface of the loch, never to be seen again.

She rearranged the basket and cloak in her arms to make room for the rubbish she had picked up, tossing the offending items into a large receptacle behind her parents' house when she finally reached it. The house was handsome to look at, and finer made than the nearby farmhouses. Red stone and slate, with painted windowsills and a sweeping garden that circled all around the building. Sorcha loved it; it had been in the Darrow family for as long as anybody could remember. Now it was almost all that remained of their wealth.

Generations ago the Darrows had been far richer than they were now. They were the landlords for the area, owning the very ground Sorcha walked upon right up through the forest and along the shore of the loch. The farmers in the area were all tenants of her father, and nobody could so much as cut down a tree or keep a boat on the loch without his permission.

But Sorcha's father was a kind man, and an understanding one. Despite outside pressure from the cities and an increased cost of living, he never raised the rent for the people who lived on his land. It was part of the reason the Darrows were much poorer now, but Sorcha was happy for it.

She could never forgive her father if he sold his principles for a more comfortable life.

Though I have to wonder why he's agreed to meet this Londoner for the third time in as many months, Sorcha thought as she crept into the kitchen as quietly as possible. She dumped her basket of brambles on the table, hung up her cloak, then used the large window overlooking the back garden to check her reflection. She looked just about as windswept and bothered as she felt, with wild hair, red cheeks and a dishevelled dress.

Sorcha knew she really should have put her hair up before going outside. She knew this, but it hadn't stopped her keeping it long and loose down her back instead. She ran her fingers through it in an attempt to tidy her appearance, wincing when she met tangle after tangle. She smoothed out her dress, splashed cold water on her face from a basin by the sink, then left the kitchen to walk down the corridor towards the parlour room.

She could hear both of her parents inside, as well as the stranger they had insisted upon Sorcha meeting today. Of course she hadn't wanted to; she had no interest in Londoners. But she was an obedient daughter, and she knew she was lucky to have parents that had not once pressured her into marriage, though Sorcha would turn twenty at the end of the month. She could be polite and lovely for this *one* Englishman.

The very notion of being lovely caused Sorcha's thoughts to return to Lachlan. It had seemed like a dream, to meet the Prince of Faeries. Sorcha had met her share of his kind before, though they tended to slip from her vision just as easily as she had laid eyes on them. On the occasions they had spoken to her they quickly gave up trying to charm her once they realised she would not give them her name.

I nearly gave it to Lachlan, though. This wasn't quite true, of course; Sorcha hadn't given him her real first name. Had she told him her surname was Darrow he could have done nothing with it. And, even then, if he knew her first name was Sorcha, he did not know her middle name.

Her father was a smart man. He had raised a clever daughter. Sorcha would not be caught be a faerie so easily.

I wanted to be caught even just for a moment, she thought despite herself, dwelling longingly on the memory of Lachlan's warm, golden skin and molten eyes. Even his braided, bronze-coloured hair had seemed to be spun of gold when the sunlight shone upon it. The silver cuff adorning one of his inhumanly pointed ears had seemed mismatched against it all, though the sapphire-encrusted piece of jewellery had been so beautiful Sorcha thought she might well have died to possess it for but a minute.

She brought her fingertips up to her lips, committing the feeling of Lachlan's mouth on hers to memory. *He kissed me like it was nothing at all. Does he go around kissing every young woman he sees whilst hanging upside down from a tree?*

It struck Sorcha that she had not taken notice of

Lachlan's clothes even once, though he had said he was going to a funeral. *Were they black?* she wondered. *I do not think so. Would faeries wear black to a funeral? What are faerie funerals like? And this was their queen. Lachlan's mother. He did not seem all that sad. Just how did she –*

"Sorcha Margaret Darrow, if you do not get in here this instant I will lock you in your room until the end of the year!"

Sorcha flinched at her mother's voice reverberating through the door. The woman had the uncanny ability to know when her daughter was lurking where she shouldn't be – which was often – and was quick to scold her. She sighed heavily, forced all thoughts of Lachlan away for another time, then fixed a smile to her face before swinging the door open.

"I'm sorry, mama, I was cleaning up by the loch-side," Sorcha apologised. Her mother clucked her tongue.

"It is not befitting a young lady to go around cleaning up filthy bottles and – look at your hair! That is no way to appear in front of a guest! Go and –"

"It's quite alright, Mrs Darrow," interrupted a low, gravelly voice. Though it was largely smoothed over with the typical accent of upper-class London that Sorcha had come to resentfully recognise from tourists, there still existed a trace of local, melodic Scots that she liked the sound of.

Out of the corner of her eye she saw her father, a mild expression on his face that suggested he did not care what Sorcha looked like. He was simply glad she had shown up at all. He inclined towards his guest with a hand.

17

"Sorcha, this is Murdoch Buchanan, a gentleman who grew up not ten miles from here before moving down to London when he was twelve. Mr Buchanan, this is my lovely daughter, Sorcha."

She withheld a wince; Sorcha did not like her real name revealed to anyone but her closest friends, despite the fact her mother thought this silly. But the lessons her father had instilled in her from a young age – to be wary of strangers, for they might be faeries – very much filtered into her attitude towards tourists. And this man, Murdoch Buchanan, had already heard her full name.

Thanks, mama, she thought dully as she turned towards the man with an apologetic smile on her face, curtsying as she did so. "I am truly sorry for my appearance and my lateness, Mr Buchanan. It was an accident."

"No need to be sorry for wishing to keep the lochside clean. It is a truly beautiful place; those responsible for sullying it ought to be ashamed of themselves."

Maybe this Londoner isn't so bad. He was born around here, after all. He might not be detestable.

Sorcha allowed herself to look at the man properly for the first time. Murdoch was tall and dressed impeccably in a white shirt, dark grey tail coat with matching waistcoat, ebony trousers and shiny leather boots. His black hair grew in loose curls around his head, and his face was clean-shaven. His eyes were dark.

Not just dark, Sorcha thought. *They are as black as his hair.* They were the most striking thing about him, though Murdoch was, by anyone's measure, a very handsome man.

His impossibly dark eyes watched Sorcha intently as

she watched him. She did not know what to say; she had the most unsettling feeling that something bad was about to happen.

"Mr Buchanan is going to be staying with us for a few days, Sorcha," her mother said, dragging her daughter out of her own head.

"Why?" she asked, though she knew she could have worded the question a little more politely.

"You know things have been getting harder for us around here," her father said. "Something has to be done to preserve the area so that nothing bad can happen to us, or to the farmers. I don't want what's happening in the Highlands to occur here."

Sorcha nodded. Everyone knew about the Clearances. An icy chill ran down her spine.

"What does this have to do with Mr Buchanan staying with us?"

It was her mother who answered. She sounded excited, which was a bad thing. Margaret Darrow being excited was a very, very bad thing indeed. "Why, Sorcha," she began, standing up to envelop her daughter's hands within her own. She smiled brightly. "You are going to marry him!"

Sorcha's mind went blank. She could only stare at Murdoch Buchanan in horror. He was a Londoner. A stranger. She did not know him, nor did he know her.

Yet he had already agreed to marry her.

She took a step towards the door, then another and another.

"No," was all she said, before fleeing for her bedroom.

No, no, no.

CHAPTER THREE

Lachlan

"Lachlan, where have you been?! The ceremony ended five minutes ago!"

Ailith came rushing towards Lachlan just as he pushed open the heavy, ornate wooden doors to his bedroom, her breathtaking face full of genuine concern. When she touched his shoulder he shrugged her off.

"I consider it a blessing to have missed it," he told her. "We both know my mother herself hated funerals. Who do you think I learned to loathe them from? But she looked forward to the feasts that followed them and I'm here for that, at least."

"You didn't answer my question."

Lachlan rolled his eyes, pouring a goblet of wine from the bronze pitcher on his bedside table when he reached it. Wordlessly he handed it over to Ailith before pouring another for himself. "Here and there," he finally replied. "Nowhere of consequence."

"Lachlan –"

"The outskirts of the forest. I sat in a tree and watched the world go by. Are you happy now?"

Lachlan didn't look at the beautiful faerie as he lied. Well, it wasn't exactly a lie. Faeries could never truly lie. The human girl Clara *was* part of the world, but he hadn't simply watched her. That was a secret he had no desire whatsoever to divulge to Ailith.

I want Clara's full name, he thought longingly. *I want it now.*

"You don't seem affected by Queen Evanna's death at all."

Lachlan was struck by the sadness in Ailith's voice. Most faeries didn't wear such negative emotions on their sleeves for everyone else to see; the blue-eyed creature in front of him was different. Perhaps it was because her father died almost a decade ago, and she was yet to get over it. Perhaps she was just as emotionally impulsive as humans were. Perhaps it was something else entirely.

Either way, it was one of the reasons Lachlan had loved her so. Now, because he couldn't have her, it was one of the things he could stand least of all.

"I shall deal with my grief however I like," he said before swallowing a large mouthful of wine. He glanced at Ailith out of the corner of his eye. "Shouldn't you be consoling my beloved stepbrother, anyway? Or your future father-in-law? I'm quite certain they are both missing your company."

Ailith grimaced. "Lachlan, don't talk about your family like –"

"Those two? My family? Don't make me laugh, Ailith. Innis and Fergus are no more my family than you are."

"You don't mean that."

Lachlan lay back onto his bed, careful not to spill his wine as he did so. Ailith *wasn't* his family, but it was a cruel thing to say nonetheless. She stood in front of him, close to tears, though even in her misery she was beautiful. It was as if her pale, elegant face had been carved to display such an emotion.

His own expression softened. "You're right. I apologise. You're all I have left in the world. You know that. I'm merely...handling my grief in my own way. I didn't mean to snap at you."

Being polite was the only way the two of them managed to deal with their intimate past, though ultimately all that meant was that they ignored how they'd felt towards each other before Fergus stole her away. But that suited Lachlan just fine.

Give it a few decades and I'll forget I loved Ailith altogether.

"Speaking of Fergus," Ailith said, though her tone suggested she was bringing him up reluctantly, "he and his father were looking for you. There's a lot that needs prepared before your coronation ceremony."

He made a face. "It is still two weeks away. If they wish to speak to me they can find me themselves."

"Lachlan –"

"Alright, alright," he sighed, swinging up from his bed and waltzing over to the large, gilded mirror hanging on the opposite wall. Lachlan fiddled with his hair, inspecting the braid that crawled across the left-hand side of his scalp. After hours spent climbing in the forest he knew he could do with unravelling the braid to comb it out, but he resisted. He liked having his hair styled this way; it ensured his mother's earring was on full display. Despite this, Ailith seemed determined never to notice it, as if she knew exactly for whom it had been intended.

In the mirror Lachlan could see Ailith walking towards the door. She sighed when she saw Lachlan watching her. "You do not have to be king if you don't want to, remember."

Lachlan scoffed at such a notion. "Where did you get that idea? If I'm not king then my half-Unseelie step family will have the crown. That's almost as bad as allowing the creatures lurking deep in the lochs to take over our court."

Ailith laughed softly into her hand. "That your mother named you after the thing you so hate never fails to amuse me."

"You and me both. Though it's not the *lochs* I mislike," Lachlan corrected, fitting on a chestnut-coloured tailcoat over his loose white shirt and dark breeches. "Merely what lives in them. You know every dark thing in there hates Seelies."

"And we hate them right back," Ailith said. "Perhaps it's time to reassess such feelings. After all, both the forests and the lochs are having to fight humans nowadays."

Lachlan said nothing. He knew Ailith was right, of course, but that didn't mean he wanted to let her know she was right. Humans really were becoming a growing problem with every tree they felled, every badly-extinguished bonfire they left behind and every broken bottle abandoned upon the forest floor.

"Come find me after you've spoken with your stepfather," Ailith murmured when Lachlan joined her by the door, brushing her elegant fingers along his sleeve before leaving his room. He touched the fabric where her fingers had been.

Another few decades, Lachlan reminded himself. *Another twenty or thirty years and Ailith will not matter to me at all.* And so Lachlan left his room, once more alone, to venture down the palace corridor with his wine goblet in hand. He veered in the general direction of his mother's old chambers, where Lachlan knew he'd find both his stepfather and stepbrother.

The building wasn't so much a traditional palace as it was a network of connected rooms carved into the very forest itself. The fair folk were a vain and prideful race, so the labyrinthine home of the royal family was painfully exquisite to look upon. The very walls were aglow, lighting the way to Queen Evanna's chambers in soft, golden tones the colour of Lachlan's skin. The tunnels and hallways were perfectly curved; not a single sharp angle existed anywhere within the palace. Some days Lachlan adored this - it was beautiful, after all. Other days he detested it, for there was nowhere to hide.

Nowhere to cry, or scream, or keep secrets from one another.

"Lachlan, there you are!"

Lachlan resisted grimacing at Innis' voice. It wasn't that he hated the faerie - he hardly bothered to hate any faeries at all - but rather that Lachlan simply did not have the patience to deal with him. Innis and his son were always scheming and plotting, their silver skin and hair stark and obvious against the gold of the Seelie Court. When his mother first announced her engagement to Innis, Lachlan had been convinced the marriage was somehow a scheme concocted by the faerie himself.

But my mother would never have been so stupid to fall for an Unseelie plot. Lachlan knew this. He *knew* it, but it didn't stop him indulging in his paranoid beliefs, either.

"We didn't see you at the funeral," Fergus said, smiling slightly as he patted Lachlan on the shoulder. Lachlan hated the way he tried to act brotherly towards him. It was all a lie, that much he was sure of. After all, had Fergus ever felt even vaguely brotherly towards him then he'd never have orchestrated a betrothal to Ailith.

Lachlan was still unsure how the faerie had managed it. Ailith certainly never told him.

Perhaps she was enamoured by his silver countenance, Lachlan supposed. *It certainly looks better against her fair skin than mine does.*

"I was grieving in my own way," Lachlan replied, giving both faeries the same answer he'd given Ailith.

Innis nodded in understanding. "Whatever you need to do, I support you. We all do. In two weeks you are meant to be king, after all."

Lachlan said nothing. Fergus' hand was still on his shoulder; when he tried to shove it off his stepbrother instead moved his hand to the silver cuff on Lachlan's ear.

"This was meant for Ailith, wasn't it?" he asked, removing the piece of jewellery before Lachlan had a chance to protest. "It truly would look beautiful on her. Have you ever considered giving it to her as a betrothal gift? Or a wedding gift, perhaps?"

"I'd rather keep it to remember my mother by," Lachlan replied, on-edge from the drastic change in subject. Something was off. Wrong. He didn't know what.

Fergus held the earring up to the light, his mercurial eyes transfixed by the way the sapphires shone. "A shame," he muttered. "It really doesn't suit you. Neither does being king."

Lachlan froze. A terrible shiver ran down his spine. "Excuse me?"

"Now, now, Fergus," his father said, shaking his head in disapproval, "you can afford to be more delicate with the boy. He just lost his mother."

Lachlan bristled. "I'm not a *boy*. Fergus is barely two decades older than me."

"And it shows." Innis' face grew stony, all previous sympathies gone. "Lachlan, you must know that you are not fit to rule. You despise the Unseelie Court –"

"I do not *despise* it," Lachlan interrupted. He made to snatch his mother's earring from Fergus but he easily glided out of the way. "I merely disagree with the Unseelie King's brother being married to the Seelie Queen."

"Come now. My mother was Seelie, or have you forgotten? I spent most of my life growing up off the coast of your own land! I have always been closer to your kind than I have been to Eirian or our father."

"And that's beside the point, anyway," Fergus added on, smiling widely at Lachlan to show his vaguely pointed teeth. "Ailith and I are to be married before the month's end. The two of us would make far greater rulers than you, Lachlan."

And then it clicked. Fergus was marrying Ailith because the court adored her. He and Innis had been plotting his ascension to the throne for months.

"You killed my mother," Lachlan said, staring at Innis with all the hatred he could muster.

But the faerie shook his head. "That I did not do, nor did my son. It was Evanna's time. That Fergus would be better on the throne than you has nothing to do with your mother's death."

"So you mean to kill *me,* instead."

His stepfather shook his head once more. "Others would ask what had happened to you, and we could not lie about it. No, Lachlan, you must disappear."

He bristled at the suggestion. "As if I would leave of my own volition!"

"Oh, that we already knew and had prepared for," Fergus said. He wrapped his hand around the silver earring; Lachlan clutched at his stomach and dropped his wine glass, sending it clattering to the floor. He watched with unfocused eyes as the dark liquid within it spilled across the cream-and-gold carpet, soaking the fibres as if it were blood. Lachlan fell to his knees, then collapsed on his side; the shiver from before had become full-on convulsions, rending his insides into tiny little pieces.

He glared at the two of them, though his eyes were watering and he could barely see. "What have you – what is this? What have you done to me?!"

"Just a little magic," Fergus said, grinning. "You know, I think I'll give Ailith your earring myself. I'll tell her it's all you left behind before you ran from the forest to escape your mother's shadow. She would believe that. I think she'd even cry for you. Would you like that, Lachlan? To know she's crying for you?"

"I –" But Lachlan couldn't verbalise the rest of his sentence through the pain. His body was changing – shimmering and twisting and cracking into something else entirely. When the convulsions finally stopped Lachlan felt altogether much smaller that he had been before, and Innis and Fergus much taller by comparison.

Innis stared down at him with a grave expression on his face. "I'd suggest you run while you can. Nobody will ask if we killed a stray fox, so we will not need to lie about it."

"A fox?!" Lachlan cried out, though the words were strange in his new throat. He bolted for the closest mirror, dismayed beyond reckoning to see russet fur, dark, pointed ears and a white underbelly. His eyes were small and beady, though his golden irises remained. There were no two ways about it; his new appearance wasn't a glamour or an illusion or a trick of the light. Lachlan really was a fox. "How did you –"

"You underestimate the power of Unseelie magic, you fool," Fergus sneered. "Now run off or we really will kill you. But who knows? Maybe an owl will do the job for me."

Lachan swung his head from Innis to Fergus then back again, too shocked to feel anger or disgust. But then fear began to creep in – the kind of deep-set instinct all animals had for anything bigger or more predatory than themselves.

He ran.

Lachlan fled the palace, winding through the corridors so quickly that even the spare passers-by who weren't yet at Queen Evanna's funeral feast did not know what to make of him. He ran out through the forest, stumbling over rabbit holes and fallen branches and loose stones until he reached the very outskirts of the trees. And then he ran some more, for good measure.

When finally Lachlan slowed to a halt to fill his lungs with much-needed air he found himself in a garden to the back of a handsome red-stoned house. Though it was by the tree line it was so close to the loch that Lachlan had never ventured near it before. When he saw the shape of a human shifting behind a window he crept closer to see what they looked like, despite the fact that he was a fox and they might throw a rock his way if they saw him.

But then the figure turned to look out the window, and Lachlan felt his heart stop.

It was Clara.

CHAPTER FOUR

Sorcha

"For the last time, Sorcha, open the door!"

"Come on, dove, I know this is a surprise. Just let us explain."

"Explain what?" Sorcha demanded from her position slumped against the door. Her parents had spent the last fifteen minutes attempting to coax her out of her room; she didn't want to budge. "You've never brought up marriage before. Why now? Why so suddenly?"

There was a pause. Sorcha heard her father sigh.

"Please, Sorcha," he said, very quietly. "Let us in. This isn't a conversation to be had shouting through a door with a guest sitting two rooms away."

Sorcha bristled at the reminder. Murdoch Buchanan was indeed a *guest,* not a family friend or a man she had fancied from afar for years. So why did her parents wish for him to marry her? Realising that her curiosity was ultimately getting the better of her Sorcha dolefully got to her feet, unbolted the heavy iron lock on the door and swung it open.

Her mother's angry face greeted her; behind her mother stood her father, who looked resigned. He gave Sorcha a small smile as the two of them trailed into her room, Sorcha closing the door behind them.

"Thank you," he said. He sat on the well-made fir wood rocking chair by the window; like their dining table and the chairs that matched it, the piece of furniture had been carved by Sorcha's great-grandfather. She loved the chair dearly, though it was beginning to creak in protest whenever someone sat upon it.

Her mother fussed for Sorcha to sit on the bed, then located a brush and began untangling the knots in her daughter's hair. Sorcha knew better than to protest, so she sat in dull compliance whilst her mother went to work.

"Why now, then?" Sorcha asked again. "And why... him? Why Mr Buchanan?"

"Do you not like the look of him?" her mother cried, offended on the man's behalf. "He is so handsome, and so gentle and well-spoken! London has been very good to him. And he's *wealthy,* Sorcha –"

"So I am to be bought, then?"

Her father shook his head. "You know it isn't like that, dove. Mr Buchanan is an investor. He informed me that there are many people in the same position as him who are interested in acquiring our land and moving the farmers off it. Mr Buchanan is from here, Sorcha. He doesn't wish for that to happen. But I didn't want him to outright buy our land, either. I want to keep it in the family."

Sorcha rolled her eyes. "That *does* sound like I'm being bought, papa. You won't sell him the land but you'll give him it by selling me to him."

"Don't speak to your father like that!" her mother chastised, dragging the brush through a tangle in Sorcha's hair far harsher than necessary to drive home her complaint. "He is doing the best he can!"

"But what about what's best for me, mama? I don't want to get married! You only wish for me to marry him because you're besotted by every city-dwelling tourist who plagues –"

"Sorcha, don't speak to your mother like that."

She winced; it was rare for both her parents to admonish her in the same conversation. But Sorcha was *angry*; how could she not be? She was to be married to a stranger.

Her father looked out of the window at the dazzling afternoon sun. "Sorcha, my health isn't what it used to be. Everyone knows that. I was always planning to pass over the land to you upon your twenty-first birthday. I would feel much better if you were financially secure and in a position to look after the farmers for many years to come."

"Papa –"

"We will not force you to marry Mr Buchanan," he interrupted, voice firm. He stood up and moved to the door. "But you can at least put in the effort to get to know the man over the next few days. Your union may not be one of love, but it could be. You have to give it a chance. He is a kind one, dove. I would not wish for you to marry him if he was not."

Her father left her room then, leaving Sorcha with

her uncharacteristically quiet mother. Though her hair was smooth, shiny and tangle-free once more, her mother was still brushing through it. It was only after several more minutes of silence that she put down the brush and turned Sorcha round to face her.

"Sorcha –"

"I know," her daughter said, though her tone was miserable. "I know papa is right. I will get to know Mr Buchanan, if that is what you both wish."

Her mother smiled approvingly; she stroked the side of Sorcha's face with the back of her hand. "I know you disapprove of city folk, especially Londoners. But remember – I grew up in Edinburgh! And I didn't turn out so bad, did I?"

Sorcha averted her eyes. "Debatable."

"Such a rude daughter!"

"I wasn't aware that honesty was considered rudeness."

The two of them giggled softly. Though Sorcha and her mother were often at each other's throats they still loved each other dearly. She ultimately trusted the older woman's judgement, even if at times she did not like it.

"Come on, then," her mother said, taking hold of Sorcha's hands to pull her up from the bed and out of the room. "Mr Buchanan will be wondering what happened! I do believe that you will rather like him, once you get to know him."

"Again: debatable. But I shall at least try to act civil."

She smiled at the look her mother gave her, and kept that same smile on her face when she was brought back through to the parlour room and left alone with

Murdoch. He was sitting by the large bay window overlooking the loch, and did not notice Sorcha's presence until she nervously sat in the armchair opposite him.

"Miss Darrow," he said, eyebrow raised in surprise when he looked at her. "You brushed your hair."

Sorcha couldn't help but laugh at the comment. She ran her fingers through a lock of it, causing it to shine like burnished copper in the sunlight. "My mother did. I apologise for my reaction earlier. The news of our engagement was...unexpected, to say the least."

The hint of a smirk crossed Murdoch's lips. Sorcha thought he almost looked amused, though it could just as easily have been the man making fun of her.

Don't think like that, she thought. *Be nice. Papa likes him. He can't be that bad.*

She fidgeted with her hands in her lap, fishing for something to say. "You're from close by, then? Where did you grow up? How old are you?"

"Twenty-seven," Murdoch replied. He pointed out through the window towards the northern point of the shimmering loch outside. "I'm from further up the loch shore, where it gets narrow and deep. I used to spend all my days swimming – even when winter was approaching – but that all stopped when I moved to London."

"Why did you move?"

"My mother died, and my father took up a new position at a bank down there. He insisted I learn his trade, so it wasn't all that surprising when I ended up as an investor."

"And now you're looking to, what? Save the loch-side from other Londoners like you?"

Murdoch straightened in his chair, expression serious as he replied, "I do not think I am as similar to them as you think, Miss Darrow. If I were I'd have simply forced your father off the land, like what is happening in the Highlands as we speak."

Sorcha said nothing. It was a sobering thought, and not one she wished to dwell upon.

She looked at her hands. "So why marry me? That seems like an awful lot of effort to go to just to procure some land."

To her surprise Murdoch laughed, his voice rough and low and very much entertained by Sorcha's take on things. Sorcha still couldn't tell if he was making fun of her, which she did not like at all. "Are you implying that you mean to be difficult, Miss Darrow?" he asked, voice full of mirth. "That you will *be* a lot of effort? Because it is most certainly effort that I'm willing to put in, having now finally met you."

Sorcha darted her eyes up to the man's face, suspicious. He only laughed harder.

"You do not believe me," Murdoch said. He clasped his hands together and rested them in his lap; Sorcha watched him do so to give her an excuse not to look into his eyes. "Are you always so sceptical of compliments? You are of good birth, and bonnie to look at. You aren't afraid to speak your mind, which I like, and you clearly care deeply for the land on which you live, which I like even more."

Sorcha didn't know what to say. She'd had local lads attempt to woo her with sweet words before; it had been easy to ignore them. But she was supposed to *marry* Murdoch Buchanan. She could not ignore him, nor what he said.

"You are kind to speak of me in that way," she ended up saying, inclining her head politely. "But I must profess that I remain dutifully suspicious. I think, after a few more days of truly getting to know me, you will realise what a horrible mistake you have made."

Sorcha half expected Murdoch to laugh at the comment as he had laughed at her previous assertions. When he remained silent she raised her head to look at him. All traces of amusement had left his face, leaving only his dark, bottomless eyes staring at her with unknowable intent.

"I do not think so," he said, so quietly Sorcha wasn't sure if she had been meant to hear it. But the words unnerved her, as did Murdoch's gaze; she shot up from her seat.

"I am tired," she mumbled, averting her eyes as she curtsied slightly. "Today has been full of surprises. If you would excuse me."

Sorcha didn't give Murdoch an opportunity to respond before she marched back to her bedroom and closed the door firmly shut behind her. She began pacing upon the wooden floor, a frown of worry creasing her brow.

"He is not bad, but I don't want to marry *anyone*," she said aloud, not caring if anybody heard her. The afternoon sunshine filtered through her window, lighting dust motes on fire and warming Sorcha's skin when she passed through it.

He is not bad, but there is something wrong with him.

That she didn't dare say aloud.

Several hours later, when the sun was low in the sky

and her parents had both come and gone to see if she was hungry, Sorcha was still pacing around her room. Something felt off. Awry. She felt like she was being watched.

Is Murdoch behind the door? she wondered. She wouldn't put it past the man, despite the fact she knew very little about him. *Or is he outside, spying on me through the window somehow?*

But when she moved over to look into the garden all she could see was the russet fur of a fox where the garden met the forest. The creature was quick to hide when it spied her.

"Strange to see a fox so far out of the forest," Sorcha yawned. She felt suddenly and inexplicably exhausted, as if she had ran for days on an empty stomach. She needed to lie down. She needed to rest. She needed sleep to help her sort through everything she had learned today. But Sorcha slipped on the flat-woven rug that lay beneath the end of her bed, tumbling over her feet with a panicked cry lodged firmly in her throat.

She was unconscious before her head hit the floor.

CHAPTER FIVE

Lachlan

He hadn't meant to knock Clara out. How could he have? Until that moment Lachlan hadn't known if any of his powers remained after being transformed into a fox. But after watching Clara pace her room for hours he had not been able to resist edging across the garden to get a better look at her, and then she'd seen him, and then –

And then she collapsed to the floor, Lachlan thought, clambering up onto the windowsill to look through the glass. The girl did not seem hurt; instead, she looked incredibly peaceful. *I only thought of her a little and she fell asleep. Does this mean I can reach her in her dreams?*

Lachlan hadn't sneaked into a human's dream for years. When he was younger he'd delighted in the pastime, seducing impressionable youths and frightening old men alike. But he'd grown out of the habit after he'd honed his skills in enchantment. Invading a person's dreams seemed pitifully easy pickings compared to manipulating them when conscious.

"I need the skill now, though," he said, muttering so quietly that if anyone had seen him they would not have been aware a fox was talking. He leapt down from the window to curl up under the rose bush growing beneath the sill, careful to ensure that nobody would be able to spy his orange fur as he lay hidden there.

He closed his eyes.

As easy as breathing, he thought, and just like that he made it through.

Clara was dreaming of sunsets.

All around her were golds and scarlets and deep, dark purples, bleeding into the horizon of her dream like ink upon a canvas. The edges of the world Sorcha created shimmered and danced in the corners of Lachlan's eyes, reminding him of the way Loch Lomond reflected the late-afternoon sun. He wondered how many thousands of sunsets across the loch Clara had seen for her dream to be such a vivid, startlingly beautiful rendition of it.

Lachlan looked down at his hands and was relieved to see he was no longer a fox. Within the realms of dreams he was once more the Prince of the Seelie Court, rightful heir to the throne.

A lot of help that is, within the head of a human girl.

He took a few steps towards Clara, whose thick, dark hair tumbled down her back far more elegantly than it had done when Lachlan spied her in the woods. The burnished copper in it was even more beautiful in the sunset than it had been in the morning light – it reminded Lachlan of the dying embers of a fire. But either Clara did not notice his approach or was blithely ignoring him; going by the stillness of her frame Lachlan assumed the former.

"Your dreams are as fair as you are, Clara."

Silence followed Lachlan's remark for the duration of a heart beat. Two. Three. And then –

"I knew I would dream of you today," Clara replied, voice soft and vacant. She did not look at Lachlan.

He took another step towards her. "And why do you say that?"

"You kissed me, did you not? I sang for you and you kissed me. To not dream of you after such a thing is impossible."

Lachlan smiled at Clara's admission. When he closed the gap between them to sit beside her she merely swung her legs back and forth from her invisible perch within the sunset.

"You are not truly dreaming of me," Lachlan said, turning Clara's head to look at him with a hand on her chin. Her mismatched eyes were lovely in the fiery light, though they remained cloudy with dream-induced confusion.

She frowned. "What do you mean by that, Lachlan, Prince of Faeries?"

"I mean that you are dreaming, but you are not dreaming of me. I invaded your dream to speak to you."

"And that is all you wish to do? To speak?"

Lachlan's lips quirked at the disappointment in Clara's voice. *Just what exactly were you hoping to dream of this evening?* he mused. Clearly the young woman's mind was far from innocent. Lachlan liked that. He liked that a lot.

He stroked the line of Clara's jaw with a gentle

thumb; she closed her eyes and sighed happily. "Perhaps in another dream, when circumstances are not so dire, we can do more than simply speak," he answered. "It's an idea I wholeheartedly look forward to exploring"

Clara froze. She opened her eyes and backed away, a frown once more returning to her face. She no longer looked to be in a trance.

"You are telling the truth," she said. "You have stolen into my dream."

"The Fair Folk cannot lie, as I'm sure you know. I'm indeed telling the truth."

Clara shook her head to clear it of its previous haze. She wrapped her arms across her chest as if they might protect her from what Lachlan was going to say next. "What circumstances are so dire you had to contact me in a dream?"

"I...hadn't meant to talk to you like this," Lachlan admitted, turning his head slightly to hide his grimace, "though admittedly if I'd spoken to you as a fox things likely would have turned out –"

"A fox?" Lachlan looked back to see Clara's face aglow with curiosity, all previous suspicion immediately cast aside. "What do you mean, a fox?"

"I mean precisely that. I seem to have found myself cursed and banished by my loving stepfamily."

Clara cocked her head to one side as she considered Lachlan's ridiculous-sounding claim. He knew the look she was giving him very well. It was the look anyone gave a faerie when they were trying to work out how they had spun a lie into something they could verbalise as truth.

"It happened exactly as I said, I swear it," Lachlan insisted, though he did not know why it was so important for Clara to believe such a thing. She could not help him, after all. "I went to see my stepfather and stepbrother after my mother's funeral and they worked Unseelie magic upon me. According to them I am unfit to wear my mother's crown, so they wished to be rid of me."

Lachlan laughed bitterly. Now that he was himself once more he had the space inside him for anger. More than anger. He was furious, and humiliated, and filled with a red-hot desire for vengeance.

Clara leaned towards him, lips parted in shock. She bit her lower one before speaking; Lachlan watched her do so with hungry eyes. Even now, when he had far more important things to deal with, he wished to control the human sitting in front of him. "So how are you going to break the spell cast upon you?" she asked. "If it is Unseelie magic then –"

"Why, my best bet is to kill them, of course," Lachlan cut in, grinning viciously. "Most any kind of curse breaks when the one who cast it dies."

"And how will you do that, when you are a fox? Can you steal into *their* dreams and smother their life from the inside?"

Oh, I really do like Clara, Lachlan thought. She hadn't tried to dissuade him from his murderous aspirations for even a second. All she wanted to know was whether he was capable of fulfilling said aspirations.

He shook his head. "I'm afraid dream-weaving on another fae is impossible. Can you imagine the havoc that would wreak?"

Clara thought about this for a moment, gaze fixed on some point beyond Lachlan's head. "What can you do, then?" she wondered aloud. "Do you have any magic left within you as a fox?"

Lachlan shook his head once more, feeling all the more frustrated as he did. "Not when I'm conscious, aside from putting little humans like you to sleep. I think I only have my full powers when I am my true self." His hand glanced against Clara's; she curled her pinky finger around his as if they were children trying to comfort one another.

"Then you need your body back," she said, so matter-of-factly that Lachlan burst out laughing.

"If I had my body back, lass, then I would not need to find a way to kill my stepfather and stepbrother."

Clara said nothing. She stared at him with her strange eyes, giving absolutely nothing away about what she was thinking. Then she looked down at her hand; Lachlan had unknowingly laced their fingers together.

"Why are you telling me what happened to you, then, when it seems neither you nor I can do anything about it?"

Lachlan leaned forward until his forehead rested against Clara's. He swept her hair away from her face, relishing the sharp intake of breath she took as he did so.

"Because you sang for me," he said. "Because you did not pity me when I told you my mother had died. Because I wanted to kiss you."

And then Lachlan moved away, standing up as if to leave. He couldn't exit Clara's dream like it was a room, of course – there was no door nor window nor opening to speak of through which to do so – but he wanted to fade out of the girl's consciousness as softly as possible so as not to rouse her from her sleep.

"You're leaving now, aren't you?" Clara asked, a disappointed look upon her face. "Will I see you again?"

"If I don't run out of time, you might."

"If you –"

"You should string rowan berries across your window to stop others like me invading your dreams," Lachlan interrupted. He didn't want to think about just how *much* time he had before he became a fox forever. "I'm surprised you haven't been spirited away into the forest already, given the proximity of your house to it."

To his surprise Clara shrugged, entirely unperturbed by the notion. "No fae who lives in the forest would dare take away a Darrow straight from their bed. We've been protecting the land here for generations. I'm somewhat surprised you didn't realise whose house you had come upon, *Prince* Lachlan."

Lachlan felt somewhat foolish. For it was true that Clara's house was considerably nicer than most others in the area. If he hadn't been a fox when he first saw it he likely would have worked out exactly which family Clara belonged to. "I have never been one to steal away the local folk before," he said, in an attempt to protect his dignity. It was true, so he could say it.

But Clara was not convinced by his cover-up. "I do not think you are as clever as you believe you are, Lachlan."

"Is that so, Clara Darrow?"

Clara's eyes did not glaze over the way they should have had Lachlan's imprisonment of her name actually worked. The smirk upon her face meant she knew exactly what he'd tried to do.

"You are clearly cleverer than I believed *you* to be," he laughed, genuinely delighted by this turn of events. Clara was certainly a worthwhile opponent. "I'm assuming there's a middle name I'm missing?"

"Something like that."

"You are lucky you can lie so well, Clara," Lachlan said. He was tempted to reside within her dream for longer, despite how precious every second of time now was to him. To wheedle Clara's full name from her – to watch her try her best to keep it from him but ultimately have it accidentally slip out – would be immensely satisfying.

Clara sighed. "Lying is the one thing I wish humans could not do." She brought her knees to her chest, staring out at the horizon of her all-encompassing, never-ending sunset. "If they could not lie then I'd know what he really wants."

Lachlan's pointed ears twitched. "He?"

"Never mind. I thought you were leaving?"

"Do you want me to go?"

"I imagine what I want doesn't especially factor into your plans, Prince of Faeries."

"I guess not," Lachlan snickered. He inclined his head towards Clara, though she wasn't looking at him. "Until next time, Clara Darrow."

"Until next time, Lachlan."

When Lachlan returned to his wretched fox body a low snarl filled his throat. It felt wrong – obscene, even – to be reduced to such a form. But his conversation with Clara had helped to clear his head and set things straight.

I need only kill Innis and Fergus. I don't need my magic to do that; all I need is my wit.

He could do it. He could craft a way to kill them.

Then he'd steal Clara's full name and ensnare her forever.

CHAPTER SIX

Sorcha

When Sorcha awoke everything was dark and silent. She could not hear the loch beat upon the shore, nor the hooting of wood pigeons and owls that ruled the skies at twilight. Even the trees were quiet, the breeze that ripped through the forest during the daytime having finally died down to nothing at all.

It is very late, Sorcha decided, rubbing her head as she tried to regain her sense of reality. It was only then that she realised she was no longer sprawled across the rug on her floor. She was in bed, securely tucked beneath the sheets.

She sat up abruptly, wide awake and hyper-aware of everything around her in the space of a moment. "Who put me to bed...?" she wondered, holding a hand firmly over her chest to calm her throbbing heart. Sorcha was still wearing the dress she'd had on when she fell asleep, suggesting one of her parents had found her lying on the floor and simply moved her over to the bed without waking her.

Or maybe they did try to rouse me and I remained asleep, Sorcha thought. *Dreams brought about by faeries are clearly heavy indeed, if I have been unconscious for hours.*

Then Sorcha remembered everything from her dream and leapt out of bed. "Lachlan," she gasped, skittering across her floor to the window. She was desperate to spy the orange fur of a fox creeping through the black of night. "Lachlan, where are you?"

But there wasn't a fox in sight, and Sorcha couldn't see a single flash of movement that might have been him, either. She collapsed into her great-grandfather's rocking chair with a heavy sigh. For all Sorcha knew Lachlan had been inside her dream for mere minutes before fleeing through the forest. He could be miles and miles away from the Darrow house by now.

I want to help him.

In truth Sorcha knew she shouldn't. The faerie clearly wanted her full name to enslave her forever, which was something she very much didn't wish to happen. Even if Lachlan was charming. Even if Lachlan was beautiful. Even if Lachlan was the immortal Crown Prince of the Seelie Court, though Sorcha knew that this was the most glaring reason of them all for why she should avoid him no matter the cost. Forever might not seem so long to a faerie; to a human it was unfathomable.

He said he was running out of time, though, Sorcha thought, burying her head against her knees as she focused on each and every word Lachlan had spoken to her. *Will his curse kill him? Will he lose all sense of himself eventually? Something else?*

But it didn't matter what would happen when his

49

time ran out; only that it would. Lachlan had to kill his stepfamily to break his curse, or so he believed, whilst he still had the ability to do so.

"And what if he doesn't?" Sorcha asked the air. She shivered at the notion. For what if Lachlan was wrong, and killing his stepfather and stepbrother did nothing at all? Or what if he wasn't capable of killing them in the first place? He was a fox, after all.

So he needs his body back, Sorcha decided, getting up to light the lantern that sat on her desk. She picked it up by its heavy iron handle and brought it over to her sizable bookshelf. *There must be some way he can return to his original form for long enough to break the curse.*

Sorcha ran her forefinger along the spines of each and every one of her books. Seelie magic clearly couldn't help Lachlan, otherwise he'd have simply gone to a faerie he trusted to help him. Unseelie magic might have been able to break an Unseelie curse, but Lachlan was unlikely to find a member of their kind close by who was willing to aid him.

"Which leaves the realms of other things," she muttered, brows knitted together in concentration as she tried to find the tome that would give her the answers she sought. "Beings more powerful than faeries. Darker than the Unseelie. Creatures like..."

Sorcha dropped her lantern as she realised exactly what she - or, rather, Lachlan - needed. It clattered to the floor with an enormous thud which echoed all around the room. Outside her door she heard a wooden floorboard creak; had the noise woken someone up? Sorcha dared not breathe as she waited to see if anybody would check up on her. After a tense minute of silence she exhaled, gently picking up the lantern and placing it on top of the bookshelf to prevent her from dropping it again.

"It must be here," Sorcha whispered, resuming her search for the book she needed. It was one of her favourites – a compendium of stories about all the remarkable, wondrous and downright terrifying creatures who lived beneath the water's surface – and yet, for whatever reason, it was missing. And then she realised where it must be.

Her father's study.

The two of them enjoyed reading together in the evenings. Last sennight Sorcha had insisted upon reading her favourite fairy tales, since she loved to hear her father's deep, sonorous voice narrate the stories. The book she was looking for was definitely on his bookshelf.

Grabbing the lantern and hoisting the hem of her dress up to her knees, Sorcha crept over to her door and carefully opened it. The hallway was dark and quiet, save for the soft sounds of her father snoring a few rooms down. Sorcha's gaze lingered on the door opposite hers; it led to the guest bedroom, where Murdoch Buchanan was most likely sleeping. The door was ajar, but she couldn't hear anything, so Sorcha tiptoed down the corridor towards her father's study.

He had an expansive collection of books; it was no wonder Sorcha had learned to love reading from him. The man spent as much time as possible with his nose in a book, whilst Margaret Darrow preferred the company of real, living people. It never ceased to amaze Sorcha that her mother read so little when her husband – and daughter – read so much.

Sorcha held the lantern up to the top shelf of the first selection of books, quickly dismissing them all when she saw they were alphabetised encyclopaedias. The next shelf down was full of atlases, then books about birds, botany, fishing and a whole host of other interesting topics.

Sorcha moved to the next bookshelf, which looked far more promising. But though she found her father's favourite collections of poems – missing three volumes of Burns' work which were currently sitting on Sorcha's desk – and a large collection of fiction written in Scots, she still could not see what she was looking for.

When she was halfway through searching the third bookshelf Sorcha was so engrossed in reading the spines that she did not hear the door behind her creak open, nor the footsteps padding towards her across the soft, lush carpet.

"Is this what you're looking for?" a low, gravelly voice asked, followed by an arm reaching over Sorcha's head to grab a book sitting on the very top of the bookshelf.

"M-Mister Buchanan," Sorcha stuttered, backing away only to hit the man's chest, for he was standing right behind her. She looked up and over her shoulder at him; his dark eyes watched her with interest. "I did not mean to wake you."

He smiled softly. "I was already awake. What are you doing up, Miss Darrow?"

"I couldn't sleep."

"You did not seem to have an issue with that earlier."

There was something about the way Murdoch spoke

– or, perhaps, the way he *looked* at Sorcha as he spoke – that informed her he had been the one who carried her to bed. The skin on her forearms tingled like it was being pricked by a thousand needles. She did not like the idea of such an unknowable stranger standing in her room, holding her close whilst she was completely unaware that such a thing was happening.

Sorcha turned on the spot to face Murdoch, though standing this close to him it was difficult to look him in the eye. He was much taller than her. *And taller than Lachlan,* she thought despite herself. *Broader, too. Stronger. If it came down to a physical fight Murdoch could probably overpower him.* It occurred to Sorcha that what she had been feeling towards Murdoch since first meeting him was fear.

"I – I do recall mentioning that I was tired," she mumbled, before attempting to side-step away from the man. Murdoch held out an arm to stop her, then waved the book he'd found in his other hand.

"This was what you were looking for, am I correct?"

Sorcha looked at the book – at the beautiful script of its title, and the haunting illustration of the most dangerous creature one could find in the darkest depths of a Scottish loch.

The Kelpie, and Other Aquatic Creatures, the title read. It was precisely what Sorcha had come into her father's study to find.

She glanced up at Murdoch, nervous beyond reckoning. "How did you –"

"That bookshelf was full of ledgers," he said, pointing behind Sorcha. "I didn't imagine you were wanting to read any of them in the middle of the night.

A book of fairy stories out of your line of sight seemed much more likely."

Sorcha said nothing. Murdoch's reasoning was sound. It made sense, so why didn't she believe it? With a slightly trembling hand she took the book from him, working hard not to recoil when his fingers brushed her own.

"Thank you," she muttered, keeping her head down and sliding out of the man's way when he finally allowed her to. "Good night, Mr Buchanan."

"And you, Miss Darrow," he replied. "I hope you fall back into dreams just as easily as you did earlier." Sorcha resisted the urge to look back to see how Murdoch was looking at her. Some part of her was deathly curious, as if she was a rabbit under the piercing gaze of a hawk, or a fox.

Lachlan, she remembered, as soon as she thought of foxes. His plight pulled Sorcha out of her terrified state like a hook in her heart. *I need to help Lachlan.* Sorcha all but ran from her father's study, leaving Murdoch to stand there in the darkness by himself. When she reached her bedroom she locked her door, planted her lantern down on the windowsill and dropped into the rocking chair, riffling through the heavy book in her hands until she reached the page she was looking for.

"This is it," Sorcha whispered, eyes bright and shining with amazement as she read every word on the page. "This is it."

For kelpies, the book said, *though their true form is akin to a large, black horse, are capable of changing their shape using their silver bridle.*

Who was to say the bridle couldn't do the same for

another creature?

Abandoning her book on the chair, Sorcha wasted no time in rummaging around her room for a bag. She filled it with clothes, a blanket, a small number of coins and some camping supplies her mother had stored beneath her bed when she hadn't known where else to put them. A tent. A pot. A canister of fuel to keep the accompanying lantern lit. Spare wicks for said lantern.

"I need food," she muttered, unlocking her door in order to peer down the corridor. But Murdoch's door was open even wider than before – a warning that Sorcha understood loud and clear.

I'm watching you.

And so Sorcha retreated back into her room, deciding that she could buy some food on her journey around Loch Lomond. She tied the bag closed, changed into a clean dress and threw on her boots, lacing them up before searching for her cloak. She ran a hand over her face when she realised it was in the kitchen.

"No matter," she said, very, very quietly. "It is barely September. I will not need it."

And then she moved over to her window, fighting against its protesting hinges to fling it wide open.

You're doing this for Lachlan, Sorcha told herself, over and over again. *If it happens that finding a kelpie takes so long that Murdoch has no choice but to return to London then that's a happy coincidence.*

Sorcha barked in amusement. Of course it would be no coincidence. It didn't matter that she understood why her parents wanted her to marry the man. It didn't matter that he was handsome, and wealthy, and clearly genuinely interested in her. When she'd looked into

Murdoch's dark, fathomless eyes and felt nothing but startling, all-consuming fear Sorcha resolutely made up her mind.

She jumped over the windowsill, deftly avoiding the rose bush beneath it. She would keep to the edges of the forest until the sun came up, then she would wander the shores of the loch. She could do this. Sorcha could find a kelpie and save Lachlan.

And she would not get married, no matter the consequences. Her father would have to find another investor, and Murdoch Buchanan another bride.

CHAPTER SEVEN

Lachlan

Lachlan had been prowling around the forest all
night, counting himself lucky when he came across a
sleeping pheasant near dawn just as his stomach began
growling insistently. It had disgusted him to eat the bird
raw, feathers and all, but when his fox body reacted
greedily to every morsel he tore from the unfortunate
creature Lachlan forgot to hate himself for doing so.

It is so easy to get used to being like this, he thought.
Too easy. For after several hours of being a fox Lachlan
no longer stumbled over his feet, or struggled with his
new eyes and overwhelmingly keen senses of smell and
sound. He'd always thought faeries had great eyes and
ears; after becoming a fox Lachlan realised by
comparison just how wonderful that eyesight had truly
been...and how sub-par his hearing was. Now he could
hear the whisper-quiet scurrying of a mouse through the
underbrush twenty metres away.

"Is this how one loses themselves to the curse?"
Lachlan wondered aloud, simply to remind himself that

he still had a voice. "They give into the fox's base instincts and forget their own?" Turning a human into a fox was a fairly standard faerie curse, for the Seelie and Unseelie alike. It was an amusing way to punish or anguish a victim, knowing that they were running around desperately trying to free themselves from the curse whilst slowly succumbing to it.

But what about cursing a Seelie? Lachlan thought. *Turning a faerie into a fox is most unheard of.* Human princes, certainly. Kings, even. But never faerie royalty. Never faerie princes.

"When I get my teeth into Fergus..." he muttered, nose buried in the dirt as Lachlan followed the scent of...something. He wasn't sure what. He *was* sure, however, that Fergus had been the one to actually cast the fox curse, not his stepfather. So Lachlan would kill Fergus first, and Innis second. He wanted the wretched half-Unseelie to watch as his only child died in front of him.

"And it will be his own fault!" Lachlan growled viciously. "His scheming will be his downfall – him and bloody Fergus both!"

"Is – is someone there?"

Lachlan stilled, ruff bristling as his ears pricked up to identify the direction of the feminine-sounding voice. *To your right,* he decided, creeping beneath fallen tree branches and across the dense carpet of pine needles that covered the forest floor in search of the speaker.

"There is nobody there," another voice said. "You are hearing things." This one was definitely male – a gruff, assured kind of voice that would have convinced Lachlan himself that he was hearing things had he not known the human was wrong. For the pair of them *were* human, which was what Lachlan had been smelling. Human, not faerie, nor animal. But there was something else he could smell or, rather, sense, that was rarely found so close to humans.

Magic.

When Lachlan got close enough he used the very early morning light filtering through the trees to help him watch the strangers. The man was tall, with a heavy cloak draping over his shoulders that covered most of his frame. The woman was much shorter, with blonde hair that fell in an intricate braid to the small of her back. *Not just blonde,* Lachlan realised. *Gold. It has been enchanted.*

"Somebody *is* here," Lachlan called out, despite his fox senses begging him to run away. But he knew the pair of strangers would startle when they could not locate who had spoken, and Lachlan was still a faerie, after all. He could not resist playing with their heads a little. And he was curious about the woman's magic hair. How could he not be? It was beautiful, even to his inferior fox eyes.

But, to his extreme surprise, the man turned to face him almost immediately. Lachlan took a careful step backwards, realising that perhaps he had made a mistake trying to unnerve the strangers. "What kind of creature are you?" the man called out. "We mean no harm! We are searching for an enchanted fox. Might you be able to help us?"

"A fox?" Lachlan echoed back, even more surprised than before.

"Yes!" came the woman's excited voice. "Julian –"

"You do not give your name to their kind, you idiot!

59

How many times have I told you that?"

"But –"

"You are not from around here," Lachlan interrupted, before fighting his animal instincts once more to trot over to the pair. The woman's eyes widened in shock and delight when she spied him; the man – Julian – was unperturbed. If Lachlan still had eyebrows he would have frowned. "But you have dealt with my kind before?"

Julian nodded. "I have. My partner here has not. But you...are not the fox I am searching for." He laughed softly. "Tell me, how often do the Fair Folk turn their own kind into foxes?"

Lachlan tilted his head to one side and twitched his tail. "Our own kind? Never. It's always humans we curse in such a way."

"And yet you aren't human, are you?"

"Call me an exception."

Julian's lips quirked. "Which makes the fox I'm looking for an exception, too. He was definitely a Seelie."

"How long ago was this?"

"About...four years ago, give or take a few months," Julian replied, chewing his lip thoughtfully. "He had just been cursed. When he saw me in the forest I think he hoped I'd be able to help him."

Lachlan drew even closer, not daring to be excited but feeling his heart quicken nonetheless. "With your magic?" he asked. "Like the kind in the lovely lass' hair?"

The woman beamed at the compliment. "Julian is a

wizard from the mainland," she explained. "The strongest wizard in France. And –"

"And I was not able to help the fox," Julian interrupted, kneeling down to better look at Lachlan. His eyes had a glow to them Lachlan would have been wary of even if he'd been in his own body. "My expertise does not lie in curses, I'm afraid. The fox parted ways with me entirely disappointed. I was... hoping to find him, if I could, though I admit I likely cannot do anything for him even now."

Lachlan's spirits fell. "So you could not help me, either."

Julian shook his head. "I'm afraid not. I could try, but I might make things worse."

"Better not to do that. I hope you find your fox, wizard, and that he is not *just* a fox by now."

His female companion narrowed her eyes. "What do you mean?"

"I mean that, eventually, the one cursed succumbs to the fox's instincts," Lachlan explained. His own fate was truly beginning to sink in now that he was speaking of it out loud. "For a human it can take as little as a few days, and as long as several months, if their minds are strong. For my kind...I do not know."

"Oh, Julian, but that would be terrible!" she exclaimed, bending down to grab the man's arm in worry. Her eyes darted from his face to Lachlan's. "Can't you do anything at all to help him?"

Julian hesitated. "I...do not think it wise. Messing with magic is a dangerous business indeed, as our friend here can attest to, given his current predicament."

Lachlan snickered despite himself. "Well met,

wizard. In that case I had best be off. My time has become precious to me in a way it never was before. Be very careful exploring the forest; I'd suggest leaving if I were you."

"What do you mean by that?" Julian asked as both he and his partner stood back up, brushing off their knees as they did so.

Lachlan had already taken several steps away from them. He turned back for a moment and grinned as much as a fox could grin. "There has been a...change in management in the Court, so to speak. I should be proof enough that said management isn't particularly *nice*."

And then Lachlan was off, darting through the trees just as he heard Julian mutter, "And this is why we can't use our names around here, foolish girl!"

I like them, he realised. *They are an interesting couple. When I get my body and my throne back I shall have to seek them out. I might even resist finding out their full names and allow them to remain as they are.*

It took Lachlan a moment too long to realise he had reached the outskirts of the forest once more, stepping out of the safety of the trees and onto the rocky shore of Loch Lomond before coming to a sudden halt.

"You could be shot!" he admonished aloud, skulking back into the trees with a furtive look around to make sure he was not seen. When Lachlan was sure he was safe he surveyed the loch with distaste. He knew the kinds of creatures who lived within it. Monstrous things which lured humans and faeries alike into its depths and consumed them. Beings with magic akin to his own, but who could lie, which made them terrifying. Even 'harmless' aquatic creatures could be dangerous – the shape-shifting selkies living along the coast of Scotland had drowned more than their fair share of humans and Seelies, who were heartbroken to discover that the one they loved had disappeared beneath the waves forever.

Then Lachlan heard a familiar voice singing and forgot about the loch altogether. *Clara!* Lachlan thought. He padded across the border between the shore and the forest until he spied her, close to the water's edge. *Just what is she doing?*

Clara clambered over a shelf of limestone, dropping down to a lower part of the beach with an ease that suggested she'd spent much of her life climbing. Her voice didn't falter over a single note of her song even as she hauled herself over the next rock and jumped across to yet another. Clearly she was enjoying herself, otherwise she would be using the path beneath the trees for a far easier journey. Lachlan had to wonder what she was doing up so early, and so far from home.

Wait, if she is so far from home then for how long has she been walking? She is miles from her house! Lachlan turned his nose up to the sky; going by the angle of the sun it was nearing seven o'clock. He'd exited Clara's dream almost eleven hours ago, with no idea when Clara herself would wake up. Considering the distance she'd travelled Lachlan had to assume she'd left her house at around three in the morning.

She is up to something, he decided. *I wonder if it has something to do with the 'he' Clara mentioned before I left. The one she didn't wish to talk about.* Curiosity firmly piqued, and with Clara's song filling his ears, Lachlan felt like he almost had no choice in the matter but to follow the girl.

I will follow her and find out what she's doing, then

get back to my own problems.

It did not occur to Lachlan even once that Clara might have left her house in the middle of the night on his behalf.

CHAPTER EIGHT

Sorcha

Despite the fact she'd been trawling along the edge of Loch Lomond since the early hours of the morning – and had, for all intents and purposes, run away from home – Sorcha was feeling surprisingly spry and good-natured.

The first few hours had been spent taking the easy path around the outskirts of the forest, with moss and pine needles beneath Sorcha's feet to soften her footsteps. But as soon as the sun had risen over the horizon she'd happily taken to the shore, climbing over rocks and dropping down to small pools caused by low summer rainfall and travelling sand drifts beneath the water. Sorcha did not care when her boots soaked through, nor when the bottom third of her dress soon followed suit. She had never cared for such things.

Sorcha lived to be outside, surrounded by the loch and the forest and the sky. It was her home. It was where she belonged.

And not with the caveat that I must have a husband, she thought, tingling all over at the memory of Murdoch pinning her against her father's bookshelf. Sorcha had wondered, at the time, whether the man could have overpowered Lachlan. She had not once considered the fact that he most definitely could overpower *her.*

"Well, he did not catch me leaving, so it doesn't matter," she said happily, nodding a greeting at an elderly couple who were sitting on a stretch of sand nearby to eat their luncheon. They watched her curiously; it was not every day that a grown woman was spotted flouncing about the loch shore, on her own, without a care in the world. Sorcha knew they were wondering who on earth her parents must be, or what her husband would think if he knew where his spouse was.

I do not care. I have more important things to think about. Like my stomach. For Sorcha was empty inside, having not eaten a single thing since the brambles she'd popped into her mouth the day before – when she'd first met Lachlan. *Has it really only been a day? It feels like weeks and months and years.*

And so Sorcha finally left the shore to venture towards a path she knew twisted through the forest to a small collection of houses about half an hour away. Though she used to accompany her father in his cart when he visited the nearby settlements in order to collect rent, nobody this far out had seen Sorcha since she was fourteen or so. She trusted they would not recognise her now.

"And if they do, so what?" she petulantly demanded of a nearby duck waddling down to the loch. It quacked in response. "By the time they send word to my parents that they've seen me I will be miles away."

As she neared the houses Sorcha was stopped more than once by passers-by; sometimes concerned, sometimes surprised, always curious. She brushed them all off by saying she was local, and knew what she was doing, then rushing away before they could enquire any further about her identity. Sorcha imagined she painted quite an unusual sight, with her heavy bag thrown over one shoulder and wet, muddied dress hitched up at the waist to avoid slapping her ankles with the sodden material. Her hair had grown wild once more, too, eliminating all suggestions that it had ever been tidy.

My mother would scream if she saw me, Sorcha mused. *Considering the fact that I am missing from the house she might well be doing so already.*

She managed to procure a few well-fired bread rolls, a couple of recently-cooked sausages and a water skin full of apple cider from a small crofting farm. The farmer's wife tried to convince Sorcha to stay a while and eat her luncheon inside, though by the look on the woman's face she knew that doing so would result in Sorcha being locked in a room until the farmer could work out who her parents were.

So she ate on foot, taking the same twisted path back to the loch-side that she'd used to reach the hamlet in the first place. It was late afternoon by then, with only a few, wispy horsetail clouds to break up the sun and the sky. *It may well be a cold night, if the sky stays this clear,* Sorcha mused as she took in the expansive blue above her. *I should find somewhere to camp sooner rather than later.*

She didn't want to have to regret not bringing a cloak with her.

Sorcha didn't want to stray too far from the loch to

camp – not least because camping deep within the forest was folly indeed. And she was seeking a kelpie, after all, which resided in the loch. She'd had no luck all day in finding one, though truthfully she had no idea how to 'find one' in the first place. *This is all guesswork,* she thought. *Guesswork and blind hope. It's not as if any of the books I owned told me how to contact such a creature.*

Eventually, after another hour or two of walking, Sorcha came across a nook at the edge of the forest that still granted her a clear view of the loch. It was a good place to set up camp: soft grass upon firm ground and tall, stepped shelves of sandstone sheltering the area from the worst of any wind or rain that might build up over the next few hours.

"I do not think I will have to deal with such things tonight, though," Sorcha murmured. The early evening sun was warm and wonderful on her face as she got to work setting up her tent; there was no foreseeable threat of bad weather. She would likely have a very pleasant night's sleep.

Despite the fact she'd eaten two hours prior, as Sorcha drove pegs into the ground and stretched out the canvas material of the tent her stomach began to grumble insistently. She knew she should have bought more food when she had the opportunity, even if people *had* asked too many questions about who she was or where she was going. Tomorrow Sorcha would have to get up early and go out of her way to purchase more. She wished she'd thought to bring a fishing rod.

Sorcha glanced back at the forest. Much of it was coniferous now that she was heading north; there would be no apples to find. She might get lucky and find some bramble bushes along the edge of the trees but it wouldn't be enough to keep her hunger at bay.

The fae have their own delicious fruit trees hidden in their realm, she thought, *but I would literally go mad if I ate from them.* Sorcha had seen it at work before – once with an unfortunate local child and twice with hapless tourists. Salt was supposed to dull the effects until the fruit was out of one's system, but in all three cases simply too much had been consumed. Only the faeries themselves could take away the hallucinations and giddy insanity brought on by the fruit, and they would only do so for a price.

A price all too often impossibly high to pay.

Will the kelpie be the same? Sorcha wondered. *I know little and less of their behaviour.* For Lachlan's sake, and for her own, she had to hope the kelpie was far more amenable than the faeries who lived in the forest.

With everything set up Sorcha unrolled her blankets and piled them into the tent with her. She didn't close up the front of it, instead choosing to keep it open in order to watch the sun set over the loch as she lay there. The water was darker here than it was back in Darach, where the loch was wide and shallow. It would only continue to get narrower and deeper than this far up the northern shore.

"I can't have walked more than six or seven miles, really," Sorcha mused, for nobody to hear but herself and the kelpie, if it happened to be listening. "It's slow going walking directly on the shore instead of on the path through the forest, you know. I'm going to a lot of effort to find you."

She sighed. If she chose to continue along the eastern shore at the rate she was going then she'd reach the most northern tip of Loch Lomond in a couple of days. After that, if Sorcha still hadn't caught sight of the kelpie, she would have to walk south along the western shore of the loch and hope to find it before she looped all the way back to Darach.

"Or I could cut through the forest tomorrow and try Loch Arklet, Katrine, Chon and Ard." She frowned at the water, daring the creature inside to respond to her suggestion. "You're not the only kelpie in the area. There's supposed to be one for every loch in Scotland."

"You are *not* searching for a kelpie. Tell me you're not that foolish, Clara."

Sorcha startled at the sound of Lachlan's voice, rushing to sit up so quickly that she knocked her head on the canvas above her. She stuck her face out of the tent and darted her eyes around, searching for the faerie in fox form. "Lachlan?" she called. "Where are you, Lachlan?"

When he crept around the side of her tent Sorcha had no doubt that Lachlan couldn't quite believe what Sorcha was planning to do. *I never knew foxes were so expressive,* she thought, watching him in wonder as he padded into her tent with a face that screamed of disapproval. Then he collapsed onto her pile of blankets as if he owned the place.

A typical faerie, to act in such a way. And yet despite the fact Sorcha knew he *was* a faerie – and a prince, to boot – rather than a domesticated animal, she still struggled to resist the urge to tickle the soft, white fur of his belly when Lachlan rolled onto his back for a moment.

"What does it matter if I'm looking for a kelpie, Lachlan?" she asked him, though now that she could see the fox shape Lachlan was cursed to possess she couldn't

70

imagine his voice answering her through its mouth.

It did nonetheless.

"Of all the creatures to seek out, one *never* seeks a kelpie," Lachlan insisted, staring at Sorcha with gleaming eyes. They were lustrous, liquid gold – just as they had been when Lachlan was in his true form. "They lure humans to the loch and eat them, or have you forgotten?"

She didn't answer, choosing instead to gawk at the fox that spoke with Lachlan's voice and saw with Lachlan's eyes. It was discomfiting to watch. Bizarre. Uncanny. He stalked forwards and nipped at her heel until Sorcha yelped.

"What was that for?!" she complained, grabbing her ankle with a hand to massage the bite marks out of it. "Forgive me for finding the voice of a *faerie prince* coming out of a *fox* somewhat bizarre!"

Lachlan said nothing, instead patiently waiting for her to answer his question, and so Sorcha pushed aside how odd it was that she was talking to a fox and rolled her eyes. She settled into a cross-legged position a careful distance away from Lachlan and his teeth. "I do not mean to fall for the kelpie's tricks. I merely plan to –"

"To what? Ask it nicely to help you do whatever it is you want to do? What *is* it you want to do, anyway? Why have you run away from home?"

Sorcha didn't answer for a long, uncomfortable moment. She felt distinctly self-conscious about the fact she'd brazenly taken on the responsibility of aiding Lachlan's plight without so much as asking him if she could. She averted her eyes, looking out towards the loch as the last of the sun's rays disappeared beneath the very edge of the dark water.

"Clara –"

"I want its bridle," Sorcha answered, too quickly. "A kelpie can change shape using it, right? So if you had it then you could –"

"Tell me you are not seeking out a kelpie on *my* behalf, you stupid girl!" Lachlan cried, getting to his feet to hiss at Sorcha. All his fur stood on end, making him twice the size he had been before.

But Sorcha could only laugh, though she didn't mean to. Now she'd gotten over her discomfort it looked ridiculous to see a fox speak with the voice of a fae, standing inside a tent and trying to intimidate her. She reached out a hand to touch his head, knowing Lachlan would likely bite her but no longer caring if he did so.

"Don't touch – Clara, will you listen to me? Go home –"

But Lachlan's voice was lost to progressively louder yips and purring noises when Sorcha began scratching behind his ears. She knocked him onto his back, indulging her reckless urge to stroke and tickle his belly.

"You have no control over me in this form," she said, delighted. "You are just a fox with the voice of a prince."

"You – Clara, this is madness!" Lachlan just barely got out. "Stop this and listen to me!"

But Lachlan's back leg was twitching the way Old Man Macpherson's collie dog did whenever she bent down to scratch her; Sorcha knew Lachlan was enjoying the attention despite himself.

"I will be careful, I swear it," Sorcha told him. "And if you are so worried about me then stay with me whilst I search."

Lachlan looked up at her from his position on his back. It reminded Sorcha of how he had swung upside down from the oak tree, and her face flushed. But the growing darkness of night hid the colour that filled her cheeks, and by the time Lachlan spoke again Sorcha's skin had grown cold.

"Your journey is folly," he said, voice quiet and serious. "You must know this. Do not endanger yourself for me."

"You wish to imprison me forever in the faerie realm," Sorcha countered. "I am no less in danger with a kelpie than I am with you."

"And yet you have chosen to help me. I do not wish to *eat* you, at the very least."

"You're right; that makes you *far* more dangerous than the kelpie."

Neither of them said anything; they were at an impasse that neither was willing to back down from. Sorcha stopped scratching Lachlan's fur and backed away.

"I will not go home even if you wish me to, Lachlan. I was the one who decided to do this, not you. You can't make me go back."

Lachlan rolled over and got up to his feet, shook out his fur and moved over to sit by her side. "Why don't you want to go home, Clara?"

"None of your business."

"That hardly seems fair," he harrumphed. "You

know what troubles me."

"That doesn't count. You came to *me* to tell me of that. I did not seek you out to bore you with human problems."

Lachlan snickered; it was a bizarre sound to hear coming from a fox's mouth. "You are certainly an intriguing one, Clara Darrow. If you insist on keeping quiet then I shall have to work even harder to make you divulge your secrets."

She gave him a side-long glance. "Does that mean you're staying with me whilst I search for a kelpie?"

"I suppose it does."

"Then get off my pillow; I'm going to sleep."

Lachlan yelped in indignation when Sorcha unceremoniously tossed him off it, before laying down and placing her own head upon it. But then he settled down against her stomach; his fur tickled Sorcha even through the thick fabric of her dress.

Lachlan tucked his tail around himself and yawned loudly. "Sleep sounds good," he agreed. "It's exhausting being a fox."

She patted his head. "Good. That means you'll let me sleep instead of crawling into my dreams."

Sorcha fought hard to calm her rapidly increasing heartbeat when Lachlan didn't reply.

CHAPTER NINE

Lachlan

"So how old are you, Clara?"

Clara lurched in surprise before she turned to face Lachlan, eyes widening at the sight of his original form. "I told you not to sneak into my dreams tonight. You said you were exhausted."

"I am," he replied, grinning at the way Clara tried to hide how pleased she was that he'd ignored her request. "But I never promised not to bother you. You do not seem all that disappointed."

Clara said nothing.

Her dream was far more muted tonight – all dark, swirling greys and foreboding, murky blues. It imitated the shallow shore of the loch at night. *Almost, but not quite,* Lachlan noted. His keen eyes spotted the subtle yet impossible ways in which the water ebbed and flowed in Sorcha's dream. Real water never moved in such a way, though one would have to sit and look upon it for hours on end to realise this.

"Do you always dream of the land around you?" Lachlan asked as he walked over to stand by Clara, who was shifting her feet through the dark water as if it were truly real.

She shrugged. "Not always. But when you live in an area full of magical, mysterious creatures it's difficult *not* to dream of it."

"I suppose that's true. Do you know why you're dreaming of the loch?"

"Because of the kelpie, of course."

"This loch seems rather dark and dangerous."

"That fits the kelpie, then."

"Yet you did not seem at all bothered by it before you fell asleep," Lachlan countered, curious about what Clara was lying to cover up. "This loch does not fit the way you think of the real one, nor the idea of a kelpie."

Clara bristled at the comment. Lachlan hadn't yet seen her lose her temper; he was interested to see what anger looked like upon her fair face. "What is it you're wanting me to tell you, Lachlan?" she demanded, before collapsing to her knees in the false water. It swirled around her without ever getting her wet, though the skirt of her dress moved as if it really was beneath the surface of the loch. "Are you really that concerned about why this dream is darker than the last?"

"Not concerned," Lachlan said, sitting down beside Clara to trickle the mysterious water through his fingers. The stuff was insubstantial – he could not feel anything at all against his skin. "Merely curious. Why did you run away from home?"

Clara stared at her knees, expression glum. There was something about the trembling of her lips that suggested she was either about to cry or rant about something. "They want me to marry."

"Who? Your parents?"

She nodded. "They've never pressured me into marriage before. Even though I'm twenty at the end of the month -"

"Thank you for finally answering my question," Lachlan cut in, smirking despite himself when Clara threw a glare his way. He thoroughly enjoyed talking to her in his actual body - one which could frown and sigh and grin and laugh the way he wanted it to.

"Do you actually want to know what is troubling me or do you merely wish to poke fun at all my silly, mortal problems?"

"They are not silly to you though, are they?" Lachlan said. "You *are* mortal. Tell me the rest of your tale and I promise not to interrupt."

Clara looked at him as if she did not believe him, though she knew Lachlan couldn't lie. She exhaled loudly, closing her eyes for a moment before sinking onto her back in the dream water. It just barely tickled her ears, causing her long hair to wind and twist around her head like a selkie's.

"There are men down in London who want to *invest* in my father's land, though we all know what that means," Clara began. She did not look at Lachlan as she spoke. "They want the farmers and villagers gone so they can do what they like with the area - chop down the forest for farmland, or turn it into their own personal hunting ground, or use the loch for one large pleasure-boat experience. We're already overrun with tourists as it is, all of them obsessed with this romantic and mostly false notion of Scotland."

Lachlan watched intently as Clara's mismatched eyes shone too brightly with barely-contained passion and rage. Clearly she'd been holding back her opinions for a while. It was fascinating to watch; even Ailith in all her emotional fragility could never dream of matching a human in the throes of anger or sadness.

Clara continued on as if Lachlan was not there beside her. "They're all in love with our 'quaint' fairy stories, and they spend a fortune buying paintings depicting them all, yet what do they do when locals warn them to be careful? They ignore us! It serves them right when they disappear without a trace or come back completely changed."

Interesting to hear a human say that about another human, Lachlan thought. He twisted his fingers through Clara's ghostly hair without being able to ever quite touch it; the water of the loch she had created was strange indeed.

"My father doesn't want anyone to lose their homes and livelihoods like they are in the Highlands," Clara said, getting back to her original point. "But the Darrow family does not have the money it once had. So he met this man from London who grew up near here." Clara glanced around as if she was back in the tent. "As in, really near here, actually. Murdoch Buchanan. He said he lived ten miles from Darach. And this man is wealthy, and an investor, but he claims he wants what's best for the area."

"You do not believe him?"

"I don't know what to believe!" Clara cried out, smashing her fists into the water in frustration. They made no sound when they hit it. "My parents wanted me to get to know him. They like him. They believe him. But my father doesn't want Mr Buchanan to outright buy the land. He wants to keep it in the family, so he wants me to marry him."

Lachlan considered this for a moment. His hand stroked against Clara's cheek as if to soothe her, though he did not remember ever *deciding* to do such a thing. "You say your parents like this Mr Buchanan," he said thoughtfully. "Does that mean you do not?"

"I –" Clara faltered. She glanced at Lachlan's long, golden fingers when they moved from her cheek to her shoulder. "I do not know if I would ever like him. I'm... scared of him."

This is interesting.

"And why is that? Because he's wealthy? Because he lives in a city? Because he –"

"No, nothing like that!" Clara protested. "I'd never be scared of someone for such superficial things, especially not when my parents asked me to give him a chance. I *wanted* to give him a chance, just for them. But I...don't know. There's something about him that terrifies me down to my very soul."

When Clara shivered Lachlan felt the vibrations of it run right through his fingers. The girl was not lying about her fear, that much was true. But Lachlan had known humans and faeries alike to be scared of that which they most desired just as often as he'd seen them terrified of monsters.

"Maybe you truly *do* like him," Lachlan muttered, so quietly Clara didn't hear him. He traced his fingers down Clara's arm to her hand; it twitched as if she wished to hold on to him.

She didn't.

"I will let you sleep," Lachlan finally said, because he did not know what else to do. But when he stood up he looked down at Clara and grinned. "If you ended up marrying this man against your will would you consider giving me your full name *then*?"

He was pleased to see a small smile curl Clara's lips. "I know better than to promise a faerie anything."

"That wasn't a no."

"Good night, Lachlan."

"Good night, Clara."

When Lachlan found himself back in his cursed fox body he felt a twinge of regret. He'd wanted to stay in Clara's dream. He'd wanted to poke and prod her to find out everything there was to know about Clara Darrow, until the biggest, darkest secret she'd ever hold inside her was that the Prince of Faeries knew her better than anyone else possibly could.

I will own all of you, Lachlan thought, taking advantage of his furred form to burrow through the folds of Clara's dress to reach beneath it. She would likely be horrified to discover that he was lying against her naked skin, though Lachlan revelled in it.

But he'd be sure to extricate himself before Clara roused from sleep. In the morning he would hunt and bring her breakfast, and then eventually she'd come to realise that a life within the faerie realm with him would be far better than some miserable arranged marriage that would suck the life and soul and voice from her.

For now, though, Lachlan truly was exhausted, so with one final glance at Clara's face he eagerly drifted off to sleep.

CHAPTER TEN

Sorcha

Several days had passed since Lachlan had decided to join Sorcha on her quest. It was more than a little bizarre to travel with a fox – not least because of the looks she received from curious passers-by. Lachlan insisted on trotting along by Sorcha's heels, though she had tried to convince him to follow her under the cover of the forest instead.

He enjoys the odd looks, Sorcha could only conclude. *He is no stranger to attention. And he likes seeing me try and act as if having a pet fox is completely normal when I come across other people.* But venturing into hamlets and villages for food with Lachlan in full view had eventually become too annoying to deal with. Sorcha had subsequently taken to wrapping a blanket around her shoulders like a shawl and hiding Lachlan inside it – an arrangement he was more than pleased with. He chose to snuggle as close to Sorcha's skin as he could possibly get, nibbling at her collarbone, pawing at her breasts and constantly trying to bother her until

Sorcha yelled at him to stop.

He is a fox, Sorcha had to keep reminding herself whenever her insides coiled up like a snake and her cheeks grew red. *There may be a beautiful faerie inside but he is still a fox. Stop getting excited.*

Lachlan had not invaded Sorcha's dreams since their first night camping together. She reasoned that it was because their days were long and hard, and he roused earlier than her every morning to go hunting for rabbits and mice and pheasants. The fresh meat helped Sorcha out immensely, and saved her rapidly-dwindling supply of money. But the early mornings and long days meant the pair of them were often so exhausted by the time Sorcha pitched her tent that they simply fell asleep before the sun finished setting, collapsed in a tangled heap together.

I do not mind, Sorcha lied. *As a fox I can get to know Lachlan better without risking him being able to work any magic upon me. Our relationship is better this way.*

That didn't stop her day-dreaming about the golden faerie prince's hand against her face whenever she had a moment to herself. She wanted that hand to rove further. She wanted him to bite at her skin and paw at her breasts as a faerie, not a fox.

"What now, Clara?" Lachlan muttered from his position swaddled against her chest, startling Sorcha out of the beginning of her dangerous day-dream. He looked obscenely comfortable; she was tempted to tip him onto the muddy ground simply to disgruntle him. Above their heads the sky was grey and heavy with low-hanging clouds. All day they had been spattered with the beginning of what promised to be a wicked bout of rain, and there was a marked chill to the air that threatened the true death of summer.

"I want to buy some bread, eggs and apple cider," Sorcha replied, indulging the fox by scratching behind his ears. "And then we should find somewhere to set up camp before the rain grows torrential."

"It wouldn't be so much of a problem if you had a cloak."

"I don't have the money to buy one and I couldn't risk taking my own with me," she replied, sighing heavily. "I told you that already."

Lachlan popped his head out of the blanket, ears stiff and twitching with interest. "And why was that, exactly?"

Sorcha pushed his head back down and out of sight; they had reached the hamlet and couldn't afford any bizarre looks thrown their way. "It was hanging up by the kitchen door. To reach it meant leaving my room and... Mr Buchanan's door was open. He'd found me browsing through my father's library for the book about kelpies half an hour before I ran away. I think he was suspicious about me being awake so late at night."

"He suspected you might run off?"

"I don't know. It doesn't matter. He never saw me leave so he can't have known where I decided to go. Now *hush* and behave yourself so the people in the market do not find me odder than I already am."

Lachlan dutifully did as he was told, which was rare.

Sorcha moved from stall to stall, pleased that she had finally come upon a hamlet when they were running a farmer's market. She bought eggs – extra for Lachlan to eat uncooked – along with venison sausages, potatoes, onions and garlic to cook in her pot. A stew was exactly the kind of thing to eat in an early autumn downpour.

But when she reached a woman selling vats of apple cider Sorcha grew nervous. People were looking at her far more frequently than usual. She wrapped her blanket a little tighter around her shoulders, ensuring that it covered most of her hair and clothes. *If I had a hood or a hat I could pass as far more anonymous than this,* she thought, frowning when she spied a couple of men around her father's age watching her intently.

"...William Darrow's girl has been missing for days," she heard one of them say.

"You think she was taken by the f-"

"Maybe," the first voice interrupted. Sorcha did not have to hear the end of the second person's question to know to whom they were referring. Her heart battered against her ribcage; she felt Lachlan press an ear against it. "I've heard rumours she was to be married, though. Might just be that she ran away."

"What do you think that means for the land?"

"I suppose it all depends on whether they find her. She must be nearing her twenties, now. I remember William bringing her with him when he did his rounds! What was her name?"

"Ah, I think it was -"

"We need to go," Sorcha muttered, resisting the urge to look at Lachlan. She scurried away from the apple cider vendor without buying any, careful to avoid looking anybody in the eye. But one of the men who had been speaking noticed her rushing off.

"Miss!" he shouted, drawing the immediate attention of everyone around him. "Miss, won't you stay and -"

84

"Sorry, I cannot stay!" Sorcha called back, practically tripping over her feet in order to leave the hamlet. She made a beeline straight for the forest, picking up the pace until she was all but running through the trees. The area around her was unfamiliar - she and Lachlan had deviated from Loch Lomond in order to explore the smaller lochs to its right for the past few days, though they'd had no success whatsoever in locating a kelpie.

But Lachlan emerged from the blanket, darting his eyes around and twitching his whiskers before saying, "Go left here then keep going straight until the trees are all pine. There is a clearing hidden away there in which we can camp away from prying eyes."

Breathlessly Sorcha obliged his directions, not daring to look behind her to see if anyone was following the pair of them. It was only when Lachlan leapt down to the ground and nodded his head that Sorcha finally stopped. Above them the rolling call of thunder warned Sorcha she did not have long to pitch her tent before the sky heaved opened and soaked her to the bone.

That afternoon, despite her shaking hands and the fear of being caught, Sorcha set up camp faster than she had ever done before.

CHAPTER ELEVEN

Lachlan

It was raining down hard upon the tent and Clara could not sleep. Lachlan was buried in the blankets, watching her as she lay there, tense, with eyes wide open. He knew that, at this rate, Clara would not get any sleep at all.

He had to distract the girl from her restlessness until her brain finally shut off.

"You constructed this tent rather well, Clara," Lachlan said, crawling out from the blankets and over her legs to inspect each and every corner of the canvas. His claws bit into her skin whenever he lingered upon it, though Clara didn't tell him to get off. "It isn't letting any wind or rain in at all."

Clara was silent for a moment. Then she sighed, blinked away the vacant look in her eyes and said, "I used to pitch it in the garden by myself when I was younger, right by the forest edge. I loved to play at camping." She kept her gaze on the pointed roof of the tent as she spoke. The rain was heavy against the material, each drop a muted thud above their heads. Every so often a gust of wind howled around the tent, too, sounding as if the world was about to end. "I had no siblings," Clara continued on quietly, "though I was never lonely doing such things by myself. I liked learning how to do new things. And besides..."

Clara turned over onto her side to face Lachlan. He sat up straight, ears and nose twitching when she cocked her head to one side and smiled softly. "A few of the local children often joined me in the tent when my parents' backs were turned. It was fun. We felt like Highland rebels hiding from the evil men who wished to send us away from our homes."

She snickered at the thought, clearly finding it childish. In truth Lachlan knew it was not so childish; it wasn't only humans who lived further north for which Clara and her friends' fantasy was very much a reality. As forests were felled and the countryside destroyed to make way for large swathes of farmland all manner of magical creatures were being pushed out alongside the humans. It was a serious, dangerous problem for all involved.

Lachlan dismissed the sobering thought for now – there was nothing he could do about it, after all.

"You know," Clara said, laughing quietly before looking away from Lachlan, "I had my first kiss on one such night in the tent, to a fiery-haired, freckled boy."

"And what became of the boy?" Lachlan asked. He crept closer to Clara until he could feel her cheek against his whiskers. She blushed, and her eyes remained averted.

"Oh, he grew up to be a fiery-haired, freckled man,"

she replied, holding her hands above her head to twist her fingers around each other. "He asked me to marry him when we both turned sixteen. I declined, of course, though my parents would have dismissed the engagement had I said yes, anyway. We were still practically children. Old Man MacPherson's son. Gregor is his name. I saw him repairing the roof of the family farm just after I met you, actually. I wonder if he still fancies me now? I hope he has moved on."

Clara spoke as if Lachlan wasn't really there, her words flowing one after the other almost as a single sentence. He had asked her, that first morning in the forest when she'd been picking brambles, if she had allowed many boys to get close to her. Clara said she hadn't; Lachlan wondered if this Gregor MacPherson kissing her in a tent was all the experience she had.

Then Clara wrinkled her nose and swung up to a sitting position. Lachlan took a few steps back in surprise. "What is wrong?" he asked.

She picked at the hem of her dress. It was filthy and damp and, Lachlan imagined, rather uncomfortable to wear. "I was so concerned about the villagers that I forgot to change into my night dress."

If Lachlan had brows to raise he would have done so. "You haven't once changed into a night dress."

"That's because my normal dresses have been dry by the time I've gone to sleep," she replied, fishing through her bag until she found the piece of clothing she was looking for. Clara smiled as she held it up and shook it out.

Lachlan circled around the material, curious. "That's not so much a dress as an overly large shirt. Very inappropriate for young ladies."

"It is one of my father's old shirts," Clara said. "I like the feeling of it."

And then, without asking Lachlan to turn away to protect her modesty, Clara deftly unfastened the front of her dress and pulled it up and over her shoulders. She slid off her stockings next – which were even filthier than her dress – leaving only a chemise to remove. Clara wasn't wearing a stays, which somehow didn't surprise Lachlan whatsoever despite it being most unheard of for a woman of marriageable age.

He could only watch agog as Clara, finally, slid out of her chemise, and though his fox eyes were not as keen as his faerie ones during the day they were excellent in the darkness. There was not a single detail Lachlan missed of the woman kneeling in front of him: he noted the curves of Clara's hips and thighs; the length of her legs; the flat planes of her stomach and the way her long, unruly hair flowed over her shoulders and covered her breasts. Lachlan was rather familiar with them, of course, given that he hid against Clara's chest whenever they were amongst other people, but he was nonetheless disappointed that her hair obscured them now.

I want to be me, he thought. There was a hunger inside him that he could not satisfy as a fox. *I want to stop Clara putting on her father's shirt with my own hands. I want to push her hair back from her face and kiss her until she's begging me to do more. I want her to tell me her name and ask that I whisk her away to the Seelie Court forever.*

"What is it, Lachlan?" Clara asked, voice carefree as if she had no idea what was going on in Lachlan's head. She was clothed once more, though the shirt barely fell below her thighs. He almost choked when he saw how exposed her legs were.

"You are killing me," Lachlan muttered, padding over to Clara and sitting in her lap before she could protest. He reached up and placed his front paws on her chest. "Lie down," he ordered. "Lie down and think of where we are."

Clara laughed at the bizarre request. "And why do you want me to do that?" She ruffled his ears; Lachlan nipped her wrist with his teeth until she pulled her hand away, wincing. "Fine," she complained. "I'll do as I'm told. There was no need to bite me, Lachlan."

"Oh, trust me, there was," he said, once more under his breath. Clara eyed him curiously but dutifully lay down nonetheless; Lachlan moved from her lap to stand overlooking her face, dipping his head down until their noses were touching. He could see his fox form within Clara's green and blue eyes and fought back a grimace. "Think of the here and now. Think of us in the tent, and the rain upon it, and the forest we're in. Keep it all in your head."

"What are you trying to do?" Clara asked in a whisper. She had grown serious once more, for which Lachlan was glad. He did not wish to spend any more time joking around.

"Just do it. Are you thinking of it?"

Clara nodded, though she still looked as if she wanted to protest. Lachlan closed his eyes, inhaled deeply, then thought of Clara – the way he had done when he'd accidentally sent her to sleep in her bedroom.

When he opened his eyes hers were closed, and her chest rose and fell beneath Lachlan's paws as if she was deep in slumber. "Good," Lachlan murmured. "Good." He leapt off Clara to slink into a corner, curling his bushy tail around him before slowing his own breathing and closing his eyes once more.

This time, when he opened them, Lachlan was himself again, and Clara was dreaming. But the tent remained around them, and the rain fell hard above them, and the night air felt cool and real and full of thunder.

Lachlan's heart rate sped up just as Clara began to rouse from where she lay. How he had missed the excitement of being himself; of using his words and his looks and his magic to get what he wanted.

"You have a talent for keeping hold of thoughts," he said, wasting no time in creeping over to Clara's side to sit by her head. She stared up at him, eyes wide in shock at his appearance. "No wonder I failed to enchant you when first we met."

"Lachlan," she began, "what are you –"

Clara's question was lost when Lachlan ran a hand through her hair to pin her to the blankets. He bent down low over her face, revelling in the way she bit her lip and tried not to avert her gaze.

He grinned.

"I think you know what I am doing."

CHAPTER TWELVE

Sorcha

One minute Sorcha was conversing with Lachlan as a fox, wishing that he was himself once more, and then the next minute her wish came true.

This is still a dream, she reminded herself. *Even if Lachlan has decided to interrupt it, and we still seem to be in the tent, this isn't real. Remember that, Sorcha. Don't forget it.*

But it was so easy to forget, when Lachlan was looking at her like that.

"This is really a dream, isn't it?" Sorcha asked. Her heart beat erratically in her chest when Lachlan's hand smoothed back her hair. "Everything looks so real."

"And yet it is indeed a dream," he replied, golden eyes and white teeth alike glinting in the darkness. He watched Sorcha intently; she squeezed her thighs together and begged for her imagination to stop running so wild.

She wanted to touch the golden-skinned faerie

leaning over her. She wanted to run her fingers along the sharp planes of his face; the braid in his hair; the points of his ears –

"Your earring," Sorcha breathed, squinting as she noticed its absence. "It is gone."

A flash of something Sorcha couldn't quite understand crossed Lachlan's inhumanly beautiful face. "Yes. Fergus – my stepbrother – took it from me to give to Ailith. Proof that I had run off and left. The bloody bastard."

Sorcha had never heard Lachlan talk in such a way. "Who is Ailith?" she asked, though she had a feeling she did not want to know the answer.

"My stepbrother's betrothed. They are to be married at the end of the month. Ailith will be Queen of the Seelie Court by his side."

"Did she...did she know what your stepfamily planned to do to you?"

To Sorcha's surprise Lachlan barked in laughter; it did not sound all that dissimilar from a fox. He shook his head. "Ailith would never do anything to hurt me, besides break my heart."

"You love her."

It wasn't a question; Sorcha was certain of it.

"I *loved* her," Lachlan corrected bitterly. "And she loved me, or at least I always thought she did. If I still love her now I do not wish to. The feeling will pass in time, as with everything."

"That is tragic," Sorcha whispered. Her eyes were full of tears, though she did not want to cry. With a gentle thumb Lachlan brushed the moisture away.

"Do not pity me," he said. He curled a hand through Sorcha's hair, lifting her head up until their lips brushed against each other. "I do not need a human to waste their emotions on me – not when their lives are so short. There are much better things you could do for me instead."

Sorcha could feel her resolve fading with each and every beautiful, carefully-chosen word Lachlan spoke to her. She knew what faeries were capable of doing to humans even without knowing their names. A cleverly-woven sentence or two could convince a person to do something they would never normally do; to indulge a dangerous whim or lie with their neighbour's wife or give all their money away. Whether Lachlan *meant* to enchant Sorcha at this specific moment in time was another thing entirely – it was possible that his magic was always at play whether he wished it or not.

When Lachlan moved away from her Sorcha sat up to face him properly. She tucked a lock of tangled hair behind her ear, regarding Lachlan with curious eyes. The faerie was wearing a long, chestnut-coloured tail coat that flowed out behind him upon the blankets. Beneath it was a white shirt that hung lazily over his frame and dark, fitted breeches. He wasn't wearing any shoes.

"Were you wearing these clothes when I first met you, Lachlan?" Sorcha asked, changing the subject so suddenly that he laughed.

Lachlan flipped his hair over his shoulder. "Yes, but not the coat. You do not remember?"

"I was rather...distracted," Sorcha admitted. "It is not your clothes that one first notices."

"That's awfully honest of you, Clara," Lachlan said, grinning wickedly. "What did you notice first, then?"

"Your hair, perhaps. Or your golden skin."

Lachlan fingered the braid that ran across the left side of his scalp. "I should unravel it. I no longer have an earring left to show off."

Another lurch of sadness filled Sorcha's stomach. Without thinking of whether it was a good idea or not she reached behind Lachlan for her bag, rummaging through it until she found a comb. "How about I plait one side of my hair to match yours, instead? That way your braid won't remind you of what you lost anymore."

But Lachlan was not listening; his gaze was on Sorcha's thighs which, because of her position stretched out towards her bag, were no longer covered by her father's shirt. Sorcha thought at first that she should protect her modesty but something insistently stopped her.

Maybe I am enchanted. I wanted Lachlan to watch me undress earlier even though he was a fox. There is something wrong with me.

But the heat roaring inside Sorcha could not be denied. It made her forget all about the villagers who had recognised her and nearly revealed her name. It made her forget about the fact her parents were no doubt looking for her. Most of all, it made her forget about Murdoch Buchanan and her sham of an engagement to him.

Sorcha wanted Lachlan, the faerie prince, no matter how dangerous giving into such a desire could be.

She stared at him staring at her. "Lachlan –"

"Let me do it," he cut in, blinking focus back into his golden eyes before removing his coat. He reached out a hand for the comb Sorcha was holding. "I will braid it."

Sorcha wordlessly complied, hesitating for only a moment before sitting herself between Lachlan's outstretched legs. His thighs were all lean muscle beneath his breeches; Sorcha gulped when she imagined feeling then intertwined with her own. Lachlan raised the comb to her scalp, and then –

"Ow!" she complained, pulling away from the comb immediately. Sorcha rubbed her head, turning to scowl at Lachlan.

He shrugged. "What did you expect? Your hair has been a mess for days."

"You're supposed to start from the bottom! That way it doesn't hurt as much."

"If you say so," Lachlan smirked, amused, pushing Sorcha back around with a hand on her shoulder. "Staying still will make it hurt less, too."

And so Sorcha forced herself not to wince and smart away every time Lachlan hit a tangle. Neither of them spoke, the only sounds around them being the soft thudding of dream rain upon the tent and the whisper of the comb through Sorcha's hair.

After a few minutes that felt, somehow, entirely endless, Lachlan finished untangling the knots in her hair and urged Sorcha to face him so that he could braid it. But he brought his knees together, deliberately not leaving enough space for her to sit between them. Despite how outrageous it was, Sorcha didn't even blink before sliding her legs over his thighs.

I am practically straddling the Prince of Faeries as he plays with my hair, she thought. *Just what am I doing? Where is this going? It's just a dream...a dream. Even if something happens it will not have truly happened. Everything is fine.*

Despite the fact Lachlan had – just barely – kissed Sorcha ten minutes ago, she felt far more self-conscious being so close to the faerie's face now than she had been before. His fingers deftly wove through the right-hand side of her hair until a braid formed, pulling one of the laces from his shirt with his teeth in order to tie it off where it curled around the back of her ear.

The opposite side from his, she thought, eyeing up Lachlan's braid as she ran a hand across her own. *I like it.*

"Much better," Lachlan murmured, putting down Sorcha's comb in order to turn her head back and forth to inspect his handiwork. "Though I imagine you'll destroy it within hours of waking up – if the braid is present at all in reality."

A noise of indignation left Sorcha's throat as she made to move away from Lachlan. But he wrapped an arm around her, squeezing her close until there was no space left between them.

Sorcha gasped at the iron of his arms. "You are strong," she said. Her hands were on Lachlan's shoulders; it was the first time she had touched him in his true form with her fingertips. The fabric of his shirt was soft and impossibly insubstantial beneath them. She thought that she'd barely have to apply any pressure at all to rip right through it.

She wanted to rip right through it.

Lachlan grazed his lips against her ear. "You are surprised that I am strong, Clara?"

Unbidden she thought of Murdoch. A chill ran

down her spine, though she shook her head and ignored it. "Not surprised," she replied, somewhat breathless by Lachlan's proximity. "Excited, perhaps."

"A good answer. Would you like to see how strong I really am?"

Lachlan's eyes glinted as he raised himself up onto his knees, placing his hands beneath Clara's thighs to lift her up with him in the process. She wrapped her legs around his waist before she could stop herself; when his fingers squeezed into her flesh Sorcha bit her lip to keep in a moan of longing.

"You almost feel as good as you do awake, Clara," Lachlan murmured. He kissed her neck; her ear; her eyelids when she fluttered them closed.

"Almost?" she whispered.

"Almost. When I have my body back I'll be sure to teach you the difference between doing such things in a dream and doing them for real."

Sorcha pulled away just enough to stare at Lachlan's mischievous face. "And what if I do not wish to?"

"One day you will stop lying to me," he laughed, "and to yourself. Trust me, you will feel much better for –"

Lachlan froze. His eyes became glass and his fingers steel against Sorcha's thighs. She frowned. "What is it?"

"I do not know. I need to wake up."

He disappeared so quickly that Sorcha was viciously thrown back into consciousness with him, disconcerted by the fact she was now lying down on the blankets in the tent, alone. In the corner Lachlan-the-fox jumped to his feet, nose held high as he sniffed the air. He burrowed through the opening of the tent and did not return for almost half an hour.

When he came back his russet fur was soaking wet. "What is out there, Lachlan?" Sorcha asked, terribly afraid. "Did those villagers find –"

"Nothing," he interrupted. Lachlan's eyes were flat and distracted. "There was nothing."

"But –"

"Just go to sleep, Clara. If I said there was nothing there was nothing."

Lachlan could not lie, which meant there really was nothing. But Sorcha was not convinced.

There is something out there. Something that bothers Lachlan. But I cannot sense it. Just what is it?

It came as no surprise that neither of them slept that night.

CHAPTER THIRTEEN

Lachlan

Rain battered Lachlan and Clara for three days before finally letting up in a bout of glorious sunshine. It brought with it the last vestiges of summer heat, which was delicious upon Lachlan's fur in combination with the new-found autumn freshness of the air. The two of them had made slow, careful progress back through the forest towards the northern point of Loch Lomond, with the intention of travelling down the western shore to the shallow southern banks. With every step he took Lachlan became certain they would not find a kelpie; there hadn't been a single sign of one so far.

The kelpies in the smaller lochs would have known we were there, looking for them. They chose not to appear. The kelpie of Loch Lomond, however...

The loch was the largest expanse of fresh water in not only Scotland but the entire British Isles. It was entirely possible that the kelpie who dwelled within it was never close enough to where Lachlan and Clara were searching to notice their presence.

But Lachlan didn't believe that for a moment. The larger the body of water, the stronger and more dangerous the kelpie. The only reasonable way the creature could not have been aware of a solitary human wandering the shores of the loch – an otherwise perfect victim to drown beneath the surface – was if it was not currently *in* the loch itself.

The idea was not so strange; the dark and twisted creatures that resided in the depths of lochs and rivers and seas often delighted in tricking humans by looking just like one of them. In that respect they were not so dissimilar from the Unseelie, who more often than not had terrible, deadly plans for the people they beguiled.

Look out for humans wearing silver chains, Lachlan told himself, over and over again. He and Clara had thankfully passed nobody on their way through the forest, but now that they were reaching the open loch shore once more Lachlan knew they had to be on their guard. *Silver chains. Silver chains. A kelpie's bridle becomes a silver chain.*

For ever since Lachlan had so very nearly indulged his desire for Clara he had not been able to shake the feeling that they were being followed. Perhaps he was being paranoid; he certainly could not *smell* anything awry. There hadn't even been the scent of a lowly human nearby for the past three days. All Lachlan had sensed were deer and birds and rabbits and, occasionally, the presence of a faerie.

A kelpie following us through the forest of the Seelie Court is impossible, Lachlan thought, trying desperately to reassure himself. *It is possible I am merely on edge because my fox senses are beginning to grow more prominent.*

Lachlan did not like that at all.

In contrast Clara seemed decidedly carefree. Now that it was clear no humans were following them she had relaxed back into enjoying their journey, revelling in the ease with which Lachlan traversed the forest as if he knew every tree, which he did. *She does not feel the same way I do,* he mused, watching as the girl nimbly jumped over a burn whilst she whistled softly. *She can't feel what it is I sensed three days ago.*

Lachlan hadn't experienced the unexplainable sensation that had frozen his entire body since. But the memory of it was there, taunting him. The only time he'd felt anything close to it had been the moment he realised Innis and Fergus had cursed him.

They cannot be following me. They can't. Maybe they sent someone out to follow me in their stead? Or is it some kind of Unseelie magic? For if it was then Lachlan had to hope that Clara's harebrained scheme to borrow a kelpie's silver bridle would somehow, miraculously, work.

When finally they broke through the trees and into the gleaming, late afternoon sunshine Lachlan and Clara were faced with a stretch of perfectly golden sand, hidden from view on two sides by sloping shelves of sandstone.

Clara tilted her head down to look at him, face bright and enthusiastic.

"Clara, we shouldn't -"

"Lachlan, it would be madness not to enjoy the sunshine for a few hours. It may be the last good afternoon we get until next year. We can spare a few hours, can't we? And besides..." Clara's gaze wandered over to the loch. Even Lachlan had to admit that the wretched, dangerous water was beautiful in the sunshine. "I would kill to bathe properly in there. My clothes could do with a soak, too."

Lachlan did not want to stop and rest. But how could he say no to Clara's request, when she was so eager? She began pouring out the contents of her bag onto a strip of grass that separated the sand from the forest before Lachlan even had a chance to nod in assent.

"We should probably camp here," she babbled excitedly. "This cove is sheltered from the elements, should it rain once more, and it is not easy for folk to spot us from the forest path if they walk along it. We can set off early tomorrow morning."

Lachlan sighed. "As you wish, Clara. Just...be careful."

He didn't know *what* she should be careful of. At this point Lachlan had to admit he didn't know anything at all. He hated it.

Clara spent the next half an hour setting up the tent, tossing Lachlan an egg which he deftly caught in his jaws when she spotted him eyeing up the last of them. They'd need to venture into a village soon to purchase more supplies, and Lachlan knew Clara was dreading it. But he didn't bring up the subject of dwindling food; it could wait until the morning.

Once their camp was set up Lachlan settled onto the sand, revelling in the warmth it had absorbed from the sun. He rolled around in the stuff for the sheer delight of doing so, causing Clara to giggle as she watched.

"It is hard to think of you as the Prince of Faeries

when you act like that, Lachlan," she said, before pulling off her boots and unbuttoning her dress. Lachlan remained as baffled by the girl's lack of modesty as he had been three days ago, especially now that her stockings and chemise joined her dress on the sand. Clara was left standing naked upon the shore of Loch Lomond for all the world to see.

"Do you not care if somebody spots you, Clara?" Lachlan asked, genuinely curious about her answer.

She shrugged. "There is nobody around but you and me. And you are a fox. Why should I worry?"

"I am a fox *now*," he muttered, whipping his tail back and forth in frustration as Clara sauntered to the edge of the loch.

Despite Lachlan's assertion that she would ruin the braid in her hair in mere hours, Clara had ensured it stayed perfect. Perhaps it was to spite him. Perhaps it was because it had survived crossing over from unconsciousness to reality – a small, inconsequential fragment of Lachlan's magic capable of surviving a dream. It kept Clara's face clear when a gust of wind battered the beach, billowing the rest of her hair behind her.

In the sunlight Clara's pale skin looked even paler than it had done in the forest. It was the typical colouring of the Celts, including the burnished copper highlights in her dark hair. Lachlan wondered if she ever tanned at all or if the freckles on her arms and face merely absorbed all the sunlight beating down upon her. *How much sunshine would she need to be as dark as me?* The thought amused Lachlan to no end.

Clara turned back to grin at him. Water lapped at her toes, breaking against them in a wave of white foam.

"Care to join me, Lachlan?" she called over. She rubbed the length of her forearms with her hands – physical proof that the loch was, most definitely, very cold.

"Never in a thousand years shall I swim in there," he asserted. Clara rolled her eyes, shrugged her shoulders once more, then ran straight into the loch without a care in the world. "Madness," Lachlan muttered. "She is absolutely mad."

But Lachlan had to admit that it was fun to watch Clara swim in the loch. She was clearly enjoying herself, dipping below the surface only to leap back up to smooth her hair back and close her eyes to the sun. When she lay back to float on the water he remembered how Clara's hair had looked in her dark, dream loch. How it had swirled around Lachlan's fingers without ever touching it.

"If I had my true form now I would join her in there," he informed the sky, in direct contradiction to what he had only just told Clara herself. "I'd swim by her side and then Clara would know that I truly wished for her to join the Court."

But despite the fact Clara had responded eagerly to Lachlan's advances in her dream back in the forest, there was something holding her at bay from him still. *If she does not come with me willingly when I have my own body back then I really will have no choice but to seek out her name.*

For under no circumstances was Lachlan going to allow Clara to live out the rest of her life as a human. He couldn't fathom the idea of her living for a handful of decades – likely fewer years than Lachlan had already lived – only to die old and grey and miserable. He could give Clara a life worth the brightness she held within her.

Lachlan spent so long thinking about Clara that he did not realise he could no longer hear her splashing about in the loch. He stood up, shaking himself of sand in order to creep towards the edge of the water. "Clara?" he said, wondering where on earth she was. No doubt she had dived beneath the surface to see how long she could hold her breath; Lachlan knew humans often enjoyed challenging themselves in such a way.

A minute passed. Two. Three.

"Clara?" Lachlan shouted, uncertainty colouring his voice. Something was wrong. Dreadfully wrong. His body began to grow cold until he could no longer move it – the same feeling that had crept up on him in Clara's dream.

"Oh, no," Lachlan cried, before leaping into the loch without another thought.

Oh, no. Oh, no. Oh, no.

CHAPTER FOURTEEN

Sorcha

Sorcha revelled in the feeling of the loch upon her skin. The bracing water tingled and stung her every nerve at first; it was much colder in the northern, deeper depths of the loch than it was in Darach's shallow shores. But then Sorcha got used to the temperature and the tingling disappeared, leaving behind a feeling of clarity and contentment as she floated on the surface like the otters she had once witnessed on a trip to the coast.

How I have missed this, she thought, closing her eyes and smiling as the sun beat down upon her face. For Sorcha swam in Loch Lomond most days between late April and early September, and the fact she hadn't done so for an entire week felt like part of her very soul had been ripped away from her.

"Especially in the forest," Sorcha murmured. "I could not live in the forest forever whilst avoiding the loch."

For of course she had been thinking about what it

would be like to live in the Seelie Court as she and Lachlan carved their way through the forest. Between his advances in her dreams and the way he watched her every move as a fox Sorcha knew the faerie had every intention of convincing her to live amongst his kind.

"I should be flattered," she told a duck when it swam close to her. "It's not very often that adult humans get taken away to the faerie realm to live with them." It occurred to Sorcha as she watched the bird that most every duck and swan and migrating goose that lived around the loch knew all her secrets – not having any siblings ultimately meant that the wildlife in the area were her closest friends. The duck quacked at her, wondering for a moment whether Sorcha had any food, before paddling on by.

She sighed. Living in the Court would be dangerous indeed. If she went willingly then she would be bound by her promise to reside there and could never leave. And if Lachlan went ahead and found out her name...

Well, it would be him that would not let me leave. Just what exactly does he want with me?

That was the crux of the matter, of course. Sorcha could not possibly know what the Prince of Faeries wanted with a mere human. He liked her voice, and he liked the look of her, and clearly he found some amusement and interest in conversing with her. But was Lachlan really so shallow as to imprison Sorcha within the faerie realm for such superficial reasons?

"Absolutely," Sorcha muttered, dunking her head beneath the surface of the loch as if it could scrub her head clean of such thoughts. After Lachlan told her about Ailith she was left with no doubt that he was capable of deep, unrelenting love. But it was also apparent that Lachlan did not revel in such emotions. It did not matter that Sorcha longed for him to return to his original form – to hold her in his arms and allow her to get lost in them. Faeries were still overwhelmingly frivolous, hedonistic creatures.

Sorcha could not live among them.

I wonder if Lachlan will let me live as I am if I'm successful in procuring the kelpie's bridle, she thought. But what did that mean for Sorcha, ultimately? A marriage to a man who scared her in order to protect the livelihood of everyone who lived around the loch? Perhaps taking Lachlan up on his offer of living in the Seelie Court would not be so bad...if Sorcha could set some conditions for her living there.

"Do not do that."

Sorcha froze. Blindly she turned her head left and right in the water, trying to see who had spoken to her. The voice was masculine and soft. Low and impossibly clear. More melodic than anything Sorcha had ever heard before. Considering she was currently underwater she had no clue how she'd heard such a voice. Sorcha darted up to the surface, gasping back a large mouthful of air before diving into the dark, swirling loch once more.

"Who is there?" she asked, the question coming out as bubbles and garbled, incoherent fragments of words.

"You have been seeking me out. Why?" the voice asked her. Beneath Sorcha the water seemed almost solid for a moment – a huge, night-dark shape closing in on her until, in the blink of an eye, it was gone.

Sorcha held her knees to her chest in order to sink a little further into the loch where the shape had been.

109

The water was clear, for it was free of the silt and sand and peat that often clouded the southern shore. She could see as far as the sunlight above her was capable of illuminating, which meant Sorcha could see nothing at all, for nothing was there.

"You are the kelpie," she said with certainty, the words once more a stream of bubbles exiting her mouth. Sorcha's heart twisted painfully in her chest; she was scared, and excited, and torn between fleeing for her life and diving ever deeper into the loch. But if this truly was the kelpie then she could not afford to lose him, so Sorcha forced herself to stay exactly where she was.

To her left the water grew solid once more. "You need not waste your breath on speaking," he said. "I can hear your thoughts. You need my help to save a faerie?"

Sorcha nodded emphatically. *I need your bridle,* she thought in the direction of his voice. *Just for a day or two. I will give it back, I swear.*

The kelpie laughed. It was a beautiful, terrible sound, reverberating all around Sorcha until it filled her mind and blocked out everything else. "Why should I help a member of the Seelie Court? They hate anything that comes from the water. Don't you want me to help *you* instead?"

There is...I do not think you can help me with my problems, Sorcha replied. She was beginning to grow faint and light-headed; she needed to breathe. But just as she kicked up towards the surface the shadowy, indistinct shape of the kelpie slid past her skin, and Sorcha forgot all about her lungs crying out for air.

"You underestimate what I can do, human," the kelpie said. When he brushed past Sorcha again she saw a flash of silver and just a hint of his dark, fathomless eyes, but as soon as she tried to focus on them they disappeared.

Do not touch him, Sorcha thought, remembering the stories from her father's book whilst temporarily forgetting that the kelpie could hear her thoughts. *I will not be able to let go. I will die.*

"Only if I wish to kill you," he replied, laughing once more. Sorcha felt a nudge against her back; she twisted around to try and catch sight of the kelpie to no avail. "And I do not wish to kill you," he continued. "Just tell me what you want."

I want to save Lachlan.

All around Sorcha the water stilled. "...the prince? Lachlan, Prince of Faeries?"

Yes! Sorcha thought, excited by the kelpie's response. *His Unseelie stepfamily cursed and banished him so they could take the throne from him. They –*

"That changes things completely."

Sorcha lit up at the kelpie's answer. *You will help him? You will lend him your bridle?*

"...in a manner of speaking," he replied. "Tell me, what is this curse that has been placed upon the prince?"

He –

But then something sharp and vicious bit at Sorcha's wrist, pulling her out of her conversation with the kelpie. "Lachlan!" she cried out when she spied the fox's orange fur turned green in the water. His name upon her lips used up the last of the air in Sorcha's lungs; she scrabbled at her throat with her fingernails as she began to sink.

Lachlan glared at her with his golden eyes before

pushing at her chest with his head, urging Sorcha towards the surface. She was dimly aware of the kelpie's presence dissipating as she desperately kicked and clawed through the loch; when Sorcha finally broke the surface there was no evidence left of his presence at all. She drew in a shuddering breath the instant she could, the air stinging her lungs like a thousand knives. It warned Sorcha of just how close to drowning she had been.

"You *idiot!*" Lachlan barked at her, incandescent with rage as the two of them struggled back to shore. "You careless, stupid human!" Had he been dry his fur would have stood on end to punctuate his anger, Sorcha knew. As it was Lachlan looked small and drenched and pitiable.

"He can – help," Sorcha breathed, barely managing to crawl onto the sand before collapsing onto her chest. "Kelpie said he can...help."

Lachlan bit her shoulder. "Don't lie down here! Get back to the tent. For the love of the forest *get back to the tent.*"

It took Sorcha every ounce of effort to move forwards, the sand below her scratching and sticking to her skin as she slid across it. When she reached the strip of grass in front of the tent Sorcha could move no further. All her strength had been drained.

Furious, Lachlan shook out his fur and bolted into the tent, dragging a blanket behind him and throwing it over Sorcha using his teeth. "Dry off and get in the – Clara? Clara!"

But Sorcha couldn't move; she'd fallen asleep.

CHAPTER FIFTEEN

Lachlan

"What is wrong with you?!"

Lachlan wasted no time invading Clara's dream in order to drop his tirade down upon her. All around him the landscape was blank – grey and dull and nondescript. Had Lachlan not sneaked inside Clara's head she likely would not have dreamed at all.

She looked at him from her position kneeling on what Lachlan could only assume was the 'floor' of her dream, blanket wrapped around her shivering shoulders as she took several deep breaths.

"He will help us," Clara stammered, fighting to vocalise each and every word.

Lachlan went bug-eyed in disbelief, flailing his arms wildly in anger. "You almost *died,* Clara! Just how stupid are you? The kelpie tried to kill you!"

"It is my own fault I almost drowned," Clara replied in earnest. She stood up, shaking slightly on her legs before finally managing to straighten herself. Her braid had come undone, unravelling over her shoulder and dripping water down the blanket. Lachlan wondered if it had also come undone in real life or whether it was merely part of Clara's dream.

He took a step towards her. "The only reason you were drowning is because the kelpie had enchanted you. Would you have spent so long underwater had it not kept you there?"

But Clara shook her head at Lachlan's explanation. "He didn't enchant me! We were talking. He was going to help. He was –"

"If it was going to help it would not have brought you so close to death!" Lachlan spat. "How can you not see that? It was twisting you around its proverbial finger because that's what kelpies like to do. They toy with their food. Surely you must know this?"

"But we were only –"

"Talking. *Talking.* Do you know how easy it is for a creature of magical birth to bend a human to its will through mere words? I think you do, Clara. I think you know this perfectly well."

Clara said nothing. She turned away from Lachlan and tightened the blanket around her body, finally aware of how exposed she was beneath it. But Lachlan closed the gap between them, grabbing Clara roughly by the shoulders in order to shake her.

"Don't ignore me!" he demanded. "You know I'm right! You *know* I am!"

"You said yourself I am not so easy to enchant," Clara protested, though she kept her eyes on her feet. "Who is to say the kelpie had any more luck than you did at weaving its will around me?"

"Look at me and find out, you ignorant human."

At first Clara did not comply. Going by the set of her shoulders she was determined not to back down from her assertion that the kelpie was actually going to help them. But, eventually, she turned around to face Lachlan properly, staring hard into his eyes with her hauntingly mismatched ones.

"I did not try all that hard to enchant you when first we met," Lachlan began, settling into a steady, poetic rhythm that would burrow quickly into Clara's mind. "Usually it takes but a mere sentence or two to ensorcell a human. It is true that you are not so ordinary. It is true that I have to put more effort into enchanting you. But I can do it, and so can the kelpie. Your will cannot keep ours shut out."

In front of him Clara's eyes began to glaze over. Her frame swayed back and forth ever so slightly, waiting patiently for his next words. Lachlan cocked his head to one side and touched the index finger of his left hand to Clara's temple. "You *want* us in your head," he continued. "You want to see with our eyes, and listen to our voices, and eat our food, and dance our dances. You long to see the darkest, most mysterious corners of the world just as much as you wish to be engulfed by the light we can create. And even if, on an ordinary day, you might not *think* you want these things, all it takes is the suggestion of magic and you will fold. Magic is magic, and humans always want what they think they cannot have. Unlace my shirt, Clara."

Of course she did as she was told – all humans did in the end. Clara's delicate fingers pulled loose the remaining lace in Lachlan's shirt, for the other had been tied into her hair, until the impossibly light fabric slipped from his shoulders to fall to the grey, never-ending ground.

"Touch me," he ordered, watching with savage delight as Clara swept her fingertips across his chest. Her eyes seemed to see right through him, or see nothing at all, as she moved her hands down to his waist. Lachlan's breathing accelerated until he could barely think.

He took hold of Clara's arms and slung them over his shoulders, causing the blanket protecting her modesty to fall. Her skin was cold and pale against his; he longed to warm it up. "Kiss me," Lachlan whispered against her lips. "Kiss me like it's all you've been thinking about from the very first moment we met. Kiss me like you want me to take you away from your dreary human life and its dreary human problems forever."

When Clara did so Lachlan eagerly dipped into the kiss. Her tongue was searing hot against his teeth, in stark contrast to her skin, and her hands crawled through his hair to pull on it, urging him closer and closer and closer.

But just as Lachlan was ready to get lost in the moment he caught sight of Clara's eyes once more. They were completely empty. Clear, lifeless glass where once her soul had been.

All her brightness was lost.

"Damn it," he muttered, pushing Clara away and bending down to retrieve her blanket. He tossed it over her shoulders before picking up his shirt and angrily putting it back on. "Damn you, Clara. Damn this farce of an alliance. Go back to your parents. I shall solve my problems on my own."

Lachlan left Clara's dream before she had the opportunity to blink life back into herself. When he returned to his fox form the sun had fully set, cooling the sand and grass and air to a decidedly autumnal temperature. Clara remained just outside of the tent, lying on the grass, covered in her blanket and so deeply unconscious Lachlan doubted even a torrential downpour could rouse her from her sleep. In his current form he was too weak to pull her back into the tent. Part of him didn't even want to.

"You are just a human," Lachlan told her, hating Clara but hating himself even more, and then he fled. Lachlan had been a fool to trust a mortal.

He would be sure never to make such a mistake again.

CHAPTER SIXTEEN

Sorcha

When Sorcha awoke it was morning. The sun shone pale and weak through a thin layer of perfectly white, even cloud, making her feel as if she hadn't quite made it back to reality yet.

"Lachlan," she uttered, though speaking his name was painful on her parched, agonised throat. Desperately Sorcha searched around for the water skin she always sat beside her at night only to realise that she was not, in fact, lying in the tent.

And she was completely naked.

"Oh my – oh my lord," she muttered, scrabbling for the blanket she had kicked off in her feverish sleep. Then Sorcha reached inside the tent and felt blindly for her water skin until her fingers found purchase on it. She drank the water down in one go, though much of the liquid escaped her lips to dribble down her chin instead.

Beads of sweat lingered upon her brow; Sorcha

wiped them away with a trembling hand. Despite the fact she was wide awake Sorcha found herself struggling to cling to her own consciousness. It unsettled her to no end that lucid, coherent thought seemed simply impossible.

Sorcha could hardly fathom what happened to her before she fell asleep, let alone what Lachlan had said and done within her dream. The whole enchanting, dangerous, alluring, wicked evening leeched away at her mind, insisting that she dwell upon it instead of the very pressing, very real issue of what she was supposed to do now that she was awake.

But one thing was for sure: Lachlan was gone.

A gust of wind carried several tangled locks of Sorcha's hair across her face. She moved them away, realising in the process that her braid had come undone.

"How was the braid even there in the first place?" Sorcha wondered, feeling stupid for not having asked Lachlan about this when she'd had the chance. He had tied it up in her dream, with the lace from his shirt, and when she had awoken the braid had remained. "He told me what happens in a dream is not truly real. So why do I have the lace from his shirt?"

Or had it, rather, Sorcha thought. She couldn't see the thin, dark strip of leather anywhere, which meant Sorcha likely lost it in the loch. She stared out at the water; it shimmered innocently beneath the weak sunshine. *Did the kelpie truly mean to kill me? He said himself that if he'd intended to do so then he would have. But I almost drowned nonetheless.*

Sorcha shivered at the memory. She never wished to experience such a raw, brutally painful experience again. Feeling her lungs collapse in on themselves was a horror unlike anything she could have ever imagined.

Lachlan was right. I'd never have stayed underwater for so long had the kelpie not enchanted me. But then...

"But then he did exactly the same thing!" Sorcha exclaimed, indignant and angry as she began to finally make sense of her dream in dribs and drabs. "He made me undress him! He made me kiss him! He – he –"

When Sorcha began to cry she detested Lachlan for what he had done all the more with each and every tear. She rubbed her hands up and down her arms over the blanket; the wool scratched her skin in the process. Sorcha wished the scratching was worse – painful enough to knock some sense back into her.

For even though she had been enchanted in her dream she had *wanted* to give in to Lachlan. She had wanted it, though the circumstances had been horrible, and he pushed her away. Something had stopped Lachlan from continuing with his dangerous game.

Sorcha doubted it was a conscience.

He told me to go home. He said he'd deal with his own problems and that I should deal with mine. I have disappointed him.

Sorcha ran her fingers through her hair until it wasn't quite so tangled for lack of anything better to do. It smelled of the loch, which twisted her insides into knots until she thought she might be sick. But it sparked the beginning of anger, too.

"The kelpie would have helped," she murmured, somehow certain of it despite Lachlan's overwhelming doubts. "He said he was going to help. I would not have been a disappointment to Lachlan had he heard our entire conversation."

120

But it was too late. Lachlan was gone, leaving Sorcha morose, alone and naked miles and miles from home. She knew she should get dressed and find the closest village in order to buy food – her stomach was painfully aware of the fact she had very little of it left to eat – but Sorcha did not have the energy within her to do anything. All she wanted to do was huddle beneath her blanket, feel the autumn wind in her hair and decidedly *not* think about how much of a failure she was.

So absorbed was Sorcha in her own helplessness that she did not hear the sound of hooves approaching, nor the whinnying of a horse as it was ushered to a stop mere feet away from her tent. It was only when the dark leather boots of its rider appeared before Sorcha's downcast eyes that she finally realised she was no longer alone.

"Miss Darrow."

Sorcha did not have to look up to know who had spoken, yet she was shocked nonetheless that the man in question now stood before her.

"Mister Buchanan," she said, very, very quietly. "I must confess that I'd rather not have to endure your company at present. Please leave."

Murdoch chuckled entirely humourlessly. "After spending four days searching for you it is highly unlikely that I'll listen to your request. The terrain around the loch hardly makes for easy riding."

"What were you hoping to achieve by finding me? It should be clear to you by now that I do not wish to marry you."

"And what were *you* hoping to achieve by childishly running away, Miss Darrow?" Murdoch countered, kneeling down upon the grass until his face was level with Sorcha's. She recoiled immediately; he squeezed her cheeks together with an iron grip that Sorcha could never hope to shake off, forcing her to look at him.

She did not want to meet his gaze. She didn't want to, but she had to. Murdoch's dark, haunting eyes were so obviously furious that Sorcha pointlessly tried to back away once more. He merely tightened his hold on her face until she gasped in pain.

"L-let go!" Sorcha stammered. "Let go! You're hurting me!"

"You want me to consider the pain I'm putting you through when you don't abide by the same consideration for others?"

"I'm *sorry* that I didn't want to marry you but there was nothing you could have said to me to make me change my -"

"I'm not talking about me!" Murdoch bit out, leaning closer to Sorcha as he spoke. She could hardly make out where his pupils ended and his irises began, but the whites of his eyes were apparent all around them. "I'm referring to your father."

Sorcha's insides froze. "My - my father? What about my father?"

"He collapsed when he realised you'd run off."

"He...is he alright? Is he -"

"I wouldn't know!" Murdoch yelled. "He was still unconscious in his bed when I decided to look for you myself. A doctor from the city was on his way to Darach when I left. Are you really so selfish that you hadn't thought of your father's poor health when you ran off? Or how your disappearing stunt would affect your mother? And for what – to sit cold, penniless and alone on some anonymous stretch of sand miles from home? Either you are a feckless, blind fool, Miss Darrow, or you are a callous and cold-hearted woman. I do not know which of those is worse, all things considered."

Sorcha went slack against his grip. She couldn't breathe. Couldn't think. Even when Murdoch eventually let her go to collapse onto the grass beside her Sorcha's sightless gaze did not waver from where his eyes had been locked on hers.

She vaguely heard him sigh. "I thought you were more mature than this, Sorcha Darrow."

Sorcha perked up at the sound of her name. She had not heard her true first name spoken aloud in a week; to hear it now – from Murdoch's lips – was odd enough to drag her back to the present. She glanced at the man. Looking closer she realised that Murdoch clearly hadn't slept much over the past few days. His curly hair was dishevelled, his boots were dull and muddy and his clothes were, for lack of a better word, decidedly ruffled.

He cast his gaze over to his horse and let out a low whistle. "Galileo, come here," he told the stallion, who raised his head from the loch's edge where he was drinking to look at his rider. The man's horse was huge in stature, with a sleek, midnight-black coat and an enviably thick, flowing mane. He was undoubtedly the most beautiful horse Sorcha had ever seen. Murdoch waved an insistent hand towards Galileo when the horse did not move until, with an impatient flick of his tail, he trotted over to the pair of them.

"Galileo?" Sorcha wondered aloud when he stopped in front of her and lowered his head. She raised a careful hand to his muzzle, stroking the soft hair there when Galileo allowed her to do so. His eyes were a deep chocolate brown; Sorcha smiled when he blinked his long lashes across them. *If it wasn't for those warm eyes he could be mistaken for a kelpie.*

"My father named him," Murdoch said, turning slightly to face Sorcha. "He was fond of philosophers and men of science."

"Was?"

"He died last month."

Galileo nudged his nose against Sorcha's cheek insistently, only stopping when she placed her forehead against his long face. She glanced at Murdoch out of the corner of her eye. "You did not tell me he passed away."

"You did not give me the opportunity to tell you."

All the anger had disappeared from Murdoch's eyes, leaving only the emptiness Sorcha had witnessed back when she first met the man. She couldn't help but wonder what had caused such nothingness to fill a person's soul, though knowing that the man's father had so recently passed away went some way in explaining it.

"...I am sorry for your loss," Sorcha murmured, looking away once more as her face flushed in shame. "And I am sorry I ran away. I truly am. You are right; it was childish and selfish of me. But I – I had my reasons."

"Reasons more important than the love you hold for your parents? For your duty to your family and to the land you profess to adore so much?"

Sorcha bristled at the accusations yet she forced her anger away. For how was she supposed to tell Murdoch about Lachlan and his curse? She somehow doubted that, after all his years living in London, he would still believe in faeries.

When Murdoch raised a hand past Sorcha's face to stroke Galileo's cheek she instinctively flinched away. "Why do you do that?" he asked, frowning at her.

"Do what?"

"Avert your eyes and avoid my touch. What have I done to scare you so?"

"I...nothing." Sorcha had no words to explain how she felt towards Murdoch – especially not now that she was beginning to realise her first impressions of him may well have been wrong. "It is nothing. I'm simply not used to –"

"Men seeking to marry you?"

Sorcha's lips twisted into the smallest of smiles at his suggestion. She risked a look at Murdoch's face; he was watching her with the same intensity that had filled his eyes the night he'd found Sorcha in her father's study.

"Strangers," she corrected. "I am scared of strangers. Particularly those from London."

Murdoch scoffed at her answer. "I *am* from here! About eight miles from this exact spot, in fact."

"No local would go about wandering the loch-side *on a horse* in such fancy clothes," Sorcha said, pointing at his boots. "You have ruined those."

"I found you, though, so I'd wager it was worth ruining a pair of shoes. And besides, the advantage of being wealthy is that it is easy to replace that which has been destroyed."

"Not all things," Sorcha muttered, thinking of her parents and, despite herself, Lachlan. "There are some things money can never repair."

Murdoch sighed heavily. Then he brushed off his coat, stood up and held a hand out to Sorcha.

"You are right, Miss Darrow," he said. "Fortunately for you, a deep-felt apology can fix what you have broken with your parents. Now, would you allow me to escort you home or will I have to tie you to Galileo and drag you back?"

Sorcha laughed softly at the ridiculous idea but quickly grew serious once more. Lachlan had told her to solve her own problems. He was right, and so was Murdoch. She couldn't keep running away or hoping that faeries and kelpies would somehow fix her life for her.

She took hold of Murdoch's hand; he tightened his fingers around hers.

"Yes, take me home if you will, Mr Buchanan."

CHAPTER SEVENTEEN

Lachlan

I can solve this. I can murder my stepfamily without my full powers. I can definitely do this.

Lachlan repeated these thoughts over and over in his head until there was nothing else left inside of him. Before his curse this would have meant ignoring his feelings for Ailith and pretending he wasn't mourning his mother's death.

Now it meant acting as if what he'd done to Clara wasn't reprehensible at all. The worst part of it was that, a week ago, he wouldn't have thought twice about the morality of enchanting a human in their sleep. It wasn't something a faerie *should* have to think about. Humans were humans, and Lachlan the Seelie Prince.

But Clara was different and he knew it.

He hated that he knew it.

Forget her, you fool. She cannot help you. She never could.

Lachlan did not know where he was going, just as he did not know what he was doing. He pelted through the forest, which grew darker and more ominous around him the deeper into its centre he went. For a moment Lachlan entertained the idea of creeping back into the central faerie realm to find a member of the Court willing to help him. Ailith, even. But something told Lachlan that both Innis and Fergus would be keeping a keen eye out for him, and that he would find no help from those otherwise most willing to grant it.

No; Lachlan was on his own.

"If only that wizard were still around," he muttered, taking a rest beneath the rotting remains of a fallen pine tree. *He might not be able to lift my curse but his magic may well be capable of dealing a fatal blow to my damned false family.* But Lachlan did not have access to his full powers, so he could not locate the man nor his charming companion. Either he picked up their scent and tracked it down to where they were or he did not find them at all. *It might be a fool's errand. I might waste too much precious time seeking them out. Fergus' coronation is a mere week away.*

Lachlan, frustrated, collapsed into a pile of blackened leaves. He rolled around in them, willing them to scratch an itch they could never reach. For what other choice did he have but to at least try and seek out the wizard? There were no other viable options left in front of Lachlan to explore.

"The girl," Lachlan said, getting back up to his feet and shaking dirt and leaves from his fur, "track the girl's scent. She was more pronounced."

He headed off in the general direction that he had first met Julian and his golden-haired partner, hoping that he could pick up a trail from the clearing where they had been looking for a faerie turned into a fox.

Well, they found one, Lachlan thought as he picked up his pace through the dense, prickly undergrowth of the forest. *I wonder how many of us there are, hiding amongst the foxes who are foxes and the foxes who were once humans. Clearly we are not as rare as I had once believed.*

And then Lachlan heard a noise that froze him to the spot in an instant. An animal crying out, clearly in dreadful pain. To hear an animal vocalise that it was hurt meant it was likely close to death and therefore no longer cared about being found by something that might eat it.

"I am hungry, I suppose," Lachlan decided aloud, swinging to his right and darting towards the source of the noise. He could not tell what kind of animal had screamed; it sounded unlike a deer or a rabbit or a pheasant. But regardless of what it was, if it was dying it would be in no position to defend itself from Lachlan and his sharp, insistent teeth.

When the animal voiced its anguish again Lachlan knew he was almost upon it. The sound was harsh and tragic in his pointed ears; he fought the urge to cringe away from it. He slowed to a soft, careful crawl when he spied the hollowed-out remains of a gnarled tree trunk from which Lachlan could hear his prey breathing, fitful and desperate. He sniffed the air; it smelled of blood and encroaching death and –

"A faerie," he gasped, leaping the final few bounds to the hollow tree to see who was lying there.

It was a fox.

The poor creature was lying on its side, struggling to breathe. Its fur was greying round the muzzle, with a tail gone limp and lifeless. Its eyes were filmy and milky-white, and crusted round the edges. It had been shot in the stomach, though going by the festering of the wound the bullet had been fired days and days ago. Lachlan wrinkled his nose at the smell of it. Every one of his fox instincts told him to run away; it was his faerie instincts that kept him rooted to the spot.

"Who are you?" he asked, taking another step or two towards the damned animal. "You are not – you are not what you seem."

The fox merely stared at him with blind, unseeing eyes. It yelped helplessly, kicking out a leg as if to warn Lachlan away. He wondered if he had mistaken the scent of a faerie, for he could no longer smell it. But then, as if the wind had changed direction, his nose picked it up once more.

"A creature of no consequence," the fox croaked out with a surprisingly melodic, masculine voice, though his mouth seemed to struggle to form the words as if he had forgotten how to speak. "A fool, even."

"But not a human. A faerie."

He nodded. "Once. But I made a mistake, and now I am a fox. In a few minutes I will be a dead one."

Lachlan bent low to nudge his nose against the fox's muzzle. "How long have you been a fox?"

"F-four years," he coughed. Lachlan backed away, for there was blood in the fox's spittle. "Four years, and with every month I have been less a faerie and more a fox. But I thought...I thought I had more time. I should have had more time."

Lachlan's heart beat painfully fast. "What do you mean, you *should* have had more time?"

The fox twisted its head to point at the wound in its stomach for a moment before burying its nose back into the dirt. "Shot," he struggled to say. "Injuries to this cursed form take more and more of yourself away. And this one...I knew I would lose myself after this. But the wound is fatal, and I am glad of it."

"There must – there must be something that can be done!" Lachlan cried, feeling bile rise in his throat as he watched the dying creature in dismay. "There *must* be something! Who cursed you?"

"I...dare not say."

Lachlan stood up as tall as he could make himself. He stared down hard upon the faerie-fox. "You are Seelie, yes?"

The animal just barely managed to nod his assent.

"Then as your crown prince and should-be king, I demand that you tell me who cursed you."

The fox's sightless, rheumy eyes grew wide. He lifted his nose towards Lachlan, sniffing at the air until he gasped. "You truly are Lachlan, the golden prince. How did you come to be this way?"

"I suspect it was the same way as you. So tell me: who did this?"

Silence. Lachlan could hear the gentle hooting of a wood pigeon upon the wind. Then the other fox shifted in the dirt and raised its head once more. "It was Innis, the Unseelie King's brother. He – I opposed his marriage to Queen Evanna. I did not trust him, nor his intentions. I do not mean to imply that our good queen did not know what she was doing in marrying him!" the fox quickly added on, to the detriment of his laboured breathing. He coughed and spluttered until his greying muzzle was stained crimson.

Lachlan licked the fox's ear. "It is alright. Speak freely."

When the fox recovered from his coughing attack he continued his explanation, though his voice was far less substantial than it had been before. "He cursed me. Innis saw that I would not stay silent on the matter. He misliked the idea that I might vocalise my opposition far more publicly at their wedding, so he cursed me."

Four years ago, Lachlan thought, feeling as if something had finally clicked into place in his head. *My mother got married four years ago. I should have worked this out the moment Julian told me of the fox he met.*

"A wizard came upon you, after you'd been cursed," Lachlan told the fox, who almost seemed to smile.

"He did. A good human, and a skilled one. But even he could do nothing for me."

"I met him a sennight ago," Lachlan said. "He was looking for you. I think he wanted to see how you were doing, though since he could do nothing to help me I doubt he'd have been able to help you now, either."

"It would have been...good to see him. But I would not want him to see me like this."

The fox whined; Lachlan lay down beside him, for he did not know what else to do. Neither of them spoke for a while, until Lachlan began to wonder if the faerie beside him had lost himself entirely.

But then he spoke once more. "My prince...you must not – please do not let Innis and his kind take your mother's crown. I fear it will be the end of all the Seelie."

Lachlan barked. "I will do everything I can to ensure that never happens. Everything. You can be sure of that."

Everything including making a deal with a kelpie, he realised. *I should not have left Clara. I should have given her idea a final try. She said the kelpie planned to help; even if it meant to fool her I could still outsmart it and steal its bridle.*

Lachlan's heart twisted at the thought. He should have gone into the loch as soon as Clara disappeared beneath the surface. He should never have left her alone in the first place. It was because of *him* that she'd almost died.

He would not make the same mistake again.

"What is your name, faerie?" Lachlan asked, turning to look at his doomed compatriot when he did not answer. In the dim twilight he could have been sleeping, but that, of course, was not the case.

The fox was dead.

Lachlan cried out in fright, jumping back as if he had been struck by lightning. For before his very eyes lay his own fate if he did not undo the curse Fergus had cast. With a final whine for the dead faerie, Lachlan turned and crashed through the rapidly-darkening forest, barely aware of the trees and ferns and birds and deer all around him as he made his way back to the shore of Loch Lomond. He *was* aware of anything that might hurt him, however, and avoided every thorn and sharp stone protruding from the ground as if his life depended on it, for it did.

It was not difficult to track Clara down; Lachlan knew her scent by heart now. But as he drew closer and closer to the fire burning down to coals outside her tent he realised he could smell something else. *Someone* else.

Clara was not alone.

CHAPTER EIGHTEEN

Sorcha

"Won't you ride upon Galileo with me, Miss Darrow?"

"Won't you give the poor creature a break and walk on your own two feet, instead?"

Sorcha didn't expect Murdoch to actually get off his horse – much less in response to such an obvious jibe – but he did. He tucked Galileo's reins beneath the saddle and patted the animal's flank gently to let him know he could wander free for a while. Galileo subsequently trotted on far ahead, pausing to chew on several mouthfuls of grass until both Murdoch and Sorcha caught up with him once more.

"Are you happy now?" Murdoch asked as they walked along the stony shore. "Walking on my own two –"

The rest of his sentence was lost to a yell as the man tripped and just barely avoided crashing to the ground. Sorcha barked out a laugh before she could stop herself.

"Have you perhaps grown too accustomed to carriages and horses from your time in London, Mr Buchanan?" she teased. "Clearly you need to spend more time using your own legs."

Murdoch ran both of his hands through his dark, curly hair whilst he regained his composure. He threw Sorcha a sly smile that she didn't entirely understand. "Clearly indeed," he said, before striding on ahead so quickly that Sorcha had to jog to try and keep up.

"Now you are being unfair!"

"You were the one who insisted I walk," he called out over his shoulder, the words accompanied by a radiant, wicked grin that could easily have rivalled Lachlan's.

Do not think about him. He is gone.

"Why are you in such a rush?" Sorcha asked when she finally reached Murdoch's side.

He raised an eyebrow at Sorcha as though the answer was obvious. "We need to find somewhere to stay the night, of course. There should be a small settlement less than a mile away, if I remember your father's maps correctly."

Sorcha looked out across the loch; the sun was low on the horizon, reflecting off the water with a dazzling brightness that she could have watched, entranced, for the rest of her life. "I would rather camp," she uttered, thinking of the kelpie. "I do not want to stay with other people right now."

When she looked at Murdoch his expression was coloured by incredulity; Sorcha fully expected him to put his foot down and march her to the closest hamlet regardless of her wishes. It was therefore to her surprise when he said, "I suppose there's no harm in camping. The weather is fair and you are clearly rather adept at it. Do you have a location in mind?"

Sorcha blinked several times before answering. "Are you...serious?"

"Only if you are. Would you like me to collect some firewood whilst you pitch the tent wherever it is you'd like to put it?"

Sorcha nodded numbly in response, wrapping her hand around Galileo's reins to pull him along with her until they found a promising stretch of grass. It was closer to the forest than it was the loch, though Sorcha could still see the water, so she was satisfied with the placement for her tent.

As the sun bled out across the horizon she began to sing the first poem that came to her head as she pitched the tent and, then, rummaged through Galileo's saddle bag for a brush to smooth out his hair. The horse whinnied and pawed at the ground in satisfaction when Sorcha began to gently brush down his face and neck, singing softly in his ear all the while.

"O can ye sew cushions,

And can ye sew sheets,

And can ye sing ballalloo when the bairn greets?

And hee and haw birdie

And hee and haw lamb

And hee and haw, birdie, my bonnie wee lamb.

And hush a –"

"I love that song."

The rest of the poem was lost to the air. Sorcha

paused in her brushing of Galileo to turn around. Murdoch had returned from the forest, arms laden with fallen branches; going by his relaxed stance and the slight smile on his face he had been listening to Sorcha for some time.

She laughed self-consciously. "It is a poem, not a song. The melody I made up last summer, when my aunt came to visit with my crying cousin." Sorcha continued brushing Galileo, reaching his flank before continuing to recount the memory. "I'd carry him – my baby cousin – to the shore and sing the lullaby until he finally quietened, and then he would sleep all night. My aunt called it a gift from God himself."

Murdoch chuckled at the notion, though he cocked his head to one side and regarded Sorcha with curious eyes. "Why does the tune sound so familiar, if you constructed it yourself?"

She shrugged. "Perhaps you happened to be visiting Loch Lomond at the time and came across me singing. It is possible; I often do not realise other people are around when I am lost in a song. Such as precisely one minute ago, for example."

Murdoch stood on the spot and thought about this for a while, then dropped the branches in his arms to the grass in order to begin constructing a fire.

"It is good that I brought extra supplies with me considering how little food you have, Miss Darrow," he murmured some time later, when the fire was crackling merrily beneath a pot of bubbling rabbit stew. "Tell me, what were you going to do when you ran out of food and money?"

Sorcha sat a respectable distance away from Murdoch before replying, "I do not know. I hadn't thought that far ahead. To be honest I hadn't thought things through at all."

A large part of me assumed I'd be living in the Seelie Court – whether I willed it or not – once Lachlan got his body back. Sorcha shivered at the thought. She had been so dreadfully careless, putting her life into the hands of a wily faerie.

"Come sit closer to the fire, Miss Darrow," Murdoch said, clearly mistaking her shiver for a sign that she was cold. Sorcha supposed she *was* cold, and she certainly did not wish to tell Murdoch what had truly caused the shiver, so she somewhat timidly inched closer to the fire – and to him.

He would think me mad if he learned the primary reason for why I ran away from home, she thought, tucking her hair behind her ear and her knees to her chest. *Never mind the fact I almost died yesterday. It feels like it was years ago.*

"What is on your mind?" Murdoch asked softly. He ladled out a portion of stew into a bowl for Sorcha; she took it with a nod and a grateful word of thanks. The steaming bowl warmed her hands and chased the chill of her near-death encounter away until it felt like a distant nightmare.

"I do not know," Sorcha replied, for in truth she couldn't pinpoint exactly what *was* on it. There was too much rattling inside her skull to isolate one single, tangible answer for Murdoch, so instead of elaborating Sorcha held the bowl of stew to her lips and took an experimental sip.

Her eyes grew bright; she stared, impressed, at Murdoch. "This is wonderful, Mr Buchanan!"

He seemed pleased by the compliment. "I enjoyed cooking with the servants down in London, especially because my father worked such long hours," he explained, twisting and turning the ladle within the pot on the fire as he did so. "He was always craving good, Scottish fare, especially when he'd been eating out most nights at his club with clients. I knew I wasn't as good a cook as my mother – she loved the kitchen so much that she'd always refused to have anyone else cook when we lived up here – but it made my father happy nonetheless that I tried to recreate her favourite recipes."

"You miss him."

Murdoch stared into the fire with an unreadable expression. Sorcha was caught between the desire to touch his arm reassuringly and back away from the glassiness of his eyes.

"One has to lose those they love, eventually," he said, more to the fire than to Sorcha. "It is an irrefutable, immutable truth. Loneliness is something you get used to, until you no longer recognise it as something that needs fixing. You simply *are* lonely, and that is that."

"That...is unbelievably sad, Mr Buchanan," Sorcha told him, the words so quiet they were almost lost entirely to the cracking of the firewood as it burned to ashes. "That is no way to live your life."

"Sometimes it is the only way, Miss Darrow. Now come, we should retire for the night. If we start up early in the morning we should reach Darach by evening. I shall change clothes outside the tent to give you some privacy as you change yours."

Sorcha was torn between following Murdoch's request to get into the tent and insisting she stay by the fire, but something told her that Murdoch would not let

140

her out of his sight for long either way. And she was tired – painfully so – which ultimately made up her mind. With a final glance at the dancing flames Sorcha retreated into the tent, quickly stripping off the layers of clothing she'd been wearing and changing into her father's shirt. She crawled beneath her favourite woollen blanket and huddled into the corner of the tent – as far away as she could get from Murdoch's huge frame when he came in to lie down behind her.

There was an awkward beat of silence. Two.

Then Murdoch snaked an arm around Sorcha's waist, causing her to yelp in fright. He pulled her towards him as if she weighed nothing at all.

"Did you really think I'd let you lie so far away, Miss Darrow?" he murmured into her ear. Sorcha tried to shift her position so that she wasn't so close to the man, but her struggle was pointless.

Murdoch was too strong.

"What do you imagine I can do two feet away from you, Mr Buchanan?" she breathed, trying once more to wriggle away from his arm to no avail.

He snickered. "Why, run away in the dead of night, of course. You have done it before, after all, when I was wide awake and watching your bedroom door. I have no doubt you could easily do it again. I'm taking no chances."

Sorcha twisted her neck around to look at Murdoch; the dim light from the dying fire outside turned his eyes to smouldering coals. She gulped. "I will not run away, I swear it."

He merely tightened his grip. "Even if you mean it, I will not let go."

She frowned. "And why not?"

Murdoch's answer was silence, though his lips twisted into the faintest hint of a smile. Resigned, frustrated and more than a little intimidated, Sorcha turned back around and closed her eyes, determined to get to sleep as quickly as possible. She had grown used to the sound of Lachlan-the-fox breathing by her head every night; having a human breathing behind her would be no different.

Except that it was, and Sorcha was achingly aware of it. Even an hour laden with fruitless attempts at sleeping later she knew that Murdoch was no more unconscious than she was. The tension in his body against hers told Sorcha he had no intention whatsoever of sleeping until he was quite certain that Sorcha herself was definitely no longer awake.

Her skin began to tingle as she thought of Murdoch, dark eyes alert and watching her. She squirmed as if she were a snake trying to shirk off its skin in an attempt to chase the uneasy feeling away.

Murdoch brought his mouth down to her ear. "I'd stop moving if I were you, Sorcha."

Sorcha bit her lip – both in response to Murdoch's solitary use of her given name and the tone in which he'd uttered it. It left no room for alternate interpretations of his current mood.

This is dangerous, Sorcha thought, a red-hot flush crawling up her skin when she found herself once more shifting against Murdoch despite his warning.

With gentle fingers, Murdoch swept Sorcha's hair away from her shoulder and kissed her neck. She sighed in response, though she hadn't meant to.

She did not know what she was *meant* to do – or want – at all.

"Are you still frightened of me?" Murdoch asked. "I cannot tell you how much I'd rather you were not." His voice was rough and low and excited, which ultimately sent a shiver of fear running down Sorcha's spine. But she was eager to feel it, and to hear more of Murdoch's enticing voice whispering in her ear. There was a pure, unbridled desire within it that held no promises of eternal imprisonment in a faerie realm. It spoke of *now*, and no consequences, and no thinking at all.

It was seductive. It was terrifying.

Murdoch's hand roamed from Sorcha's waist to her thigh, and his fingertips slid beneath the hem of her father's shirt. She did not stop him.

Am I doing this because of Lachlan? Sorcha thought, though her body was yelling at her to ignore the faerie and focus on the man who was leaving a trail of hungry kisses down her neck. *Because of what he did to me? Or because he did not trust that I could help him, and he left? Am I really so childish and reactionary?*

But in thinking about Lachlan a wave of familiar, unnatural heaviness invaded Sorcha's brain. Her eyelids fluttered. Her limbs grew slack. Her breathing slowed.

Murdoch noticed her change of state immediately. He sat up and gently pushed Sorcha onto her back. "Sorcha – Miss Darrow? What is wrong?"

But Sorcha could not answer him; she had been dragged into unconsciousness.

She did not know if she was relieved to escape the man, and what she had been about to do with him, or not.

143

CHAPTER NINETEEN

Lachlan

"Clara, I am sorry I had to put you to sleep once more –"

"What are you doing here, Lachlan?"

Clara's stare cut through Lachlan like a knife. It was obvious she was not happy to see him. He took a step towards her, almost crying with relief at having his own feet back. "Clara –"

"What do you want?"

She wasn't in the mood for any of Lachlan's usual charming, enchanting words, that much was clear. He couldn't blame her.

He lowered his head. "I am sorry, Clara Darrow. I am sorrier than I have ever been before. It is not a feeling I am used to experiencing."

A pause. "...and what, exactly, are you sorry *for?*"

"For leaving," Lachlan said, risking another step towards Clara when she did not back away. She cast her gaze up from his feet all the way to his eyes, searching for a sign that Lachlan was somehow lying. "I was angry that you'd almost died for me," he continued. "You, a human, die for *me*? For trying to help me in a situation where I could not help myself? It's pathetic."

Clara quirked an eyebrow. "Either your apology has a mind of its own or you do not sincerely wish to give it."

"I do!" Lachlan insisted. He closed the distance between them and enveloped Clara's hands in his own, squeezing them slightly too hard in his desperation for her to understand him.

Her expression grew uncertain at the gesture. "Lachlan –"

"I should never have let you go into the loch alone. You even *asked* me to join you. You asked me, and I arrogantly declined. The least I could have done to save my own skin was to get it wet in the process."

"And...is that all you're sorry for?" Clara asked, keeping her eyes on their hands as she entwined her fingers with Lachlan's. He didn't dare smile at the whispering of her skin against his, though he wanted to.

"Of course not. Of course not, Clara. What I did to you...even if I was angry and hurt and worried I should never have done what I did to you. I should never have enchanted you."

"Even though, from the very beginning, that's what you've intended to do once you have your body back?"

"That's...that's different," Lachlan muttered, averting his eyes from Clara's. He found that he could not stand to see her blue and green irises up close, so full of light and life that he had, barely a day ago, snuffed out.

"And what is that supposed to mean, Lachlan? How is it different?"

"Because one was supposed to teach you a lesson, and the other – the other..." He sighed, breaking away from Clara in order to run a hand through the unbraided side of his hair. He glanced at her; Clara was watching him with an understandably confused expression on her face, but then she frowned and crossed her arms over her chest.

"How is enchanting me forever different from what you did in my dream last night?" she asked again.

Lachlan almost laughed, for to him it was obvious. "Because I *want* you to live in the Seelie Court – with me," he said. Clara's cheeks turned pink at his admission, so Lachlan eagerly admitted to more. "I want you to live there and sing there and love the forest and adore me whilst I adore you. And I want you to be happy. Clara, a life with my kind would make you far happier than the life set out before you by your parents. You are too special for the realm of ordinary men. It –"

"You could have simply *asked* me, Lachlan."

He paused. "I did, did I not? When –"

"You asked if I would consider giving you my full name if I ended up being forced to marry Mr Buchanan," Clara corrected. "That is *not* the same as asking me if I would, of my own volition, live in the faerie realm."

Oh.

And then, to his and Clara's surprise, Lachlan *did* burst out laughing. It was a peal of genuine, good-for-his-soul laughter, so infectious that eventually Clara joined in, too. "I guess it's not in my nature to do such a

146

human thing as to ask you to do something willingly."

"You'd ask if you knew you could trick me into staying forever, with no opportunity to ever leave," Clara replied, still giggling softly.

He shrugged. "What can I say? I am a faerie. You cannot hold me to your mortal standards."

"And you cannot hold me to yours."

"Well met, Clara."

"So what do we do now?"

Lachlan sat down, for the first time taking in his surroundings as Clara knelt beside him. Her dream was dyed the colours of a burning coal; Lachlan reckoned she must have been thinking of the smouldering fire outside her tent.

"We find the kelpie," he said. He slid his hand over Clara's, a smile creeping across his lips when she once more interlaced her fingers with his. He turned his head to look at her. "But no spontaneous diving into the loch. We plan this properly."

Clara nodded. "Properly. Which means...?"

"That we need to make it show itself. We cannot deal with it as an inconsequential shape in the water."

"He," Clara corrected. Her eyes glazed over slightly. "It's a he. The kelpie, I mean."

"Should I be jealous of this kelpie, Clara?"

She rested her head on Lachlan's shoulder. "Perhaps. He does lord over the loch, my most beloved place, after all."

"I thought you loved the forest and the loch equally?"

She snickered. "I do. But you and the forest are already here, beside me. And you are jealous. A human girl could not ask for more...however dangerous a jealous faerie might be."

Clara's words were playful as if she did not take them seriously – as if she did not take Lachlan's *feelings* seriously. He guessed he could not blame her. But her assumption was not wrong; a jealous faerie was dangerous indeed.

Lachlan curled a finger beneath Clara's chin and raised her lips to his. "If I asked you now," he whispered against them, "would you say yes?"

Clara stilled. Her beautiful eyes were steady and sure. "I could not live with you the way you want me to."

"But you would consider it, on your own terms? You would?"

She smiled mischievously. Lachlan wanted nothing more than to kiss it away and make it his. "That's something to discuss once you have your body back for good, do you not think?"

"I –"

It was Lachlan's turn to freeze. For in that moment there was something off about Clara's dream. Something *familiarly* off. Lachlan could sense a darkness – a heaviness – that told him they were no longer alone.

Clara bit her lip, concerned at the change in him. "Lachlan, what is it?"

"You cannot feel it," he said, eyes wide as he watched her. It was obvious she did not know what was going on. "You cannot –"

Get out of here.

Lachlan got to his feet and looked around wildly, though he could see nothing that had not been there before. But the heaviness he could feel got even more oppressive until Lachlan could hardly stand.

Leave her alone. She is not yours.

Clara stood up and tried to touch Lachlan's arm. He shrugged her off. "Lachlan," she asked again, "what is it?"

"We –"

And then, as if he had never been anywhere else in the first place, Lachlan found himself back inside his fox body, curled up in a ball behind Clara's tent. He was being prodded with a stick.

"Get away from here, fox," urged a voice Lachlan did not recognise. He scrambled to his feet, backing away from the stick before it could hit him again. When he looked up he saw that the voice belonged to the man who had been travelling with Clara, enveloped in shadow and smoke from the remains of the fire.

"Leave before I make you wish you had," he said. Though his voice was hushed Lachlan felt as if he had shouted. "I won't have vermin near my future wife."

So this is Mr Murdoch Buchanan.

Lachlan wanted to open his mouth and tell the man that Clara did not want him. That *he* should be the one to leave. But Lachlan didn't, because right now the stranger could easily kill him. And he was a fox; he was not supposed to speak. So Lachlan did the only thing he could.

He ran.

But he would not go far, and tomorrow he would

contact Clara again.

It's time for her to stage another escape, he thought, grinning wickedly at the idea of Mr Buchanan discovering his betrothed had, once more, ran from him.

For a faerie. For Lachlan.

CHAPTER TWENTY

Sorcha

Sorcha and Murdoch were but three miles from Darach and the sun was low. Sorcha had been sat upon Galileo all afternoon – having finally given into Murdoch's insistence that she should, at least for a while, ride on the horse. Given that her muscles ached from a solid sennight of non-stop walking Sorcha was eager for the respite it gave her feet.

Murdoch was not riding with her, choosing instead to walk by Galileo's side, the horse's reins looped twice around his left hand. She wondered if he was keeping his distance because of what had transpired in the tent the night before.

He had not once asked why Sorcha had fallen unconscious.

He must be suspicious, she thought. *He found me asleep on my bedroom floor nine days ago, too. He must know that something isn't right.*

But, even so, Murdoch remained resolutely quiet on

the matter, which only served to unsettle Sorcha further. She did not let it show on her face, of course, for ultimately she had much bigger problems to deal with than what Murdoch thought of her fainting habits.

He may well be thinking that I need to see a doctor and that is all. An understandable belief, given what happened.

Sorcha's face flushed as she recalled exactly what *happened* before Lachlan had driven her to sleep. She stole a glance at Murdoch only to realise that he was staring at her. She recoiled from him, forgetting that she was on Galileo, and was only saved from falling heavily onto her back by the man's iron grip on her arm.

"Just what are you thinking, Miss Darrow?!" he exclaimed, a frown shadowing his black eyes. "You need to be careful when riding such a large horse. Have you gone mad?"

"Perhaps..." she muttered, rubbing away the marks his fingers had left on her arm as her face grew ever more crimson out of sheer embarrassment. Sorcha was a more than serviceable rider; to have slipped from a horse at her age was folly. *It shouldn't matter if Murdoch thinks me an idiot. It shouldn't. After all, I need to break away from him to help Lachlan as soon as I can. And then...*

She sighed. After having spent the past two days with him Sorcha had to admit that Murdoch Buchanan was, as her father had told her, a decent man. He was honest, well-spoken and good company. His conversation was interesting. He was more that easy to look at. And when he'd snaked a hand around Sorcha's waist, whispered in her ear and kissed her neck –

"Truly, Miss Darrow, what *are* you thinking about?"

Murdoch asked insistently. Sorcha looked away, desperately trying to calm her red and flustered appearance.

"You said you wish to preserve the area as it is," she said, voice too quick and high-pitched to convince Murdoch that she'd truthfully been mulling over such a thing, "but you are still an investor. What would you intend to do after we – *if* we – married?"

Murdoch was silent for a while, clearly deep in thought. The quiet stretched out long enough for Sorcha to regain her composure once more; by the time the man was ready to respond she found that she could look at him again.

"I suppose you are right," Murdoch said, smiling up at Sorcha. "Certainly the company I work for would expect me to get *something* out of the land."

"So you would not resign and simply...live up here?"

He laughed incredulously. "Miss Darrow, I may be wealthy but I'm not *that* wealthy. Even if I sold my father's property in London I would not have enough saved up to allow us to live a comfortable life over the next few decades without any additional income – especially when I'd have to cover the deficit for the farmers your father has been paying up to now."

It was Sorcha's turn to be silent. She had not truly thought about what it meant to protect the people who lived on her father's land. What it cost to do so, in more than money. William Darrow was tired and sick; though he loved every one of his tenants dearly they were literally taking years off his life.

"Papa never speaks to me about the financial pressure he's under," Sorcha mumbled, feeling ashamed, "even though he taught me how to do the books and how to collect the rent and made me memorise the names of each and every farmer in the area. But he avoids talking to me about anything that causes him trouble. I wish he would."

"Then perhaps you could start by not running away, to prove you are responsible and trustworthy."

Sorcha cringed at the remark but, when she caught Murdoch's eye, it became apparent he had not meant it unkindly. "You mean well," he said, "but you do not truly understand the consequences of your actions yet, nor how the world truly works. Perhaps that is your father's fault for shielding you from so much."

"I –"

"I am not criticising him," Murdoch interrupted. He scratched Galileo's neck; the horse whinnied happily. "Your father is a great man. I respect him deeply. But there are things you must learn, Miss Darrow, whether you wish to or not."

Sorcha didn't know what to say. Murdoch was right, and it brought her right back to reality after her dream the night before. Though her memory of it was hazy towards the end – Lachlan had disappeared rather abruptly – Sorcha had been left in no doubt that the faerie sincerely wished for her to leave behind her human life altogether to live with him.

Could I really do that? she wondered. *If Lachlan agreed to allow me to stay human, and to come and go as I please, could I throw away my responsibilities in order to live within the Seelie Court?*

Sorcha's gaze fell upon Murdoch once more. He ran a hand across his jaw, where several days' worth of dark stubble covered his skin. *He would not look so bad if he chose not to shave it off,* Sorcha decided. *Though it would itch like my father's beard does against my face when he kisses me.* She shook her head to chase the ridiculous thought away, horrified, before her cheeks were set on fire once more.

"To answer your original question, though," Murdoch said, cutting through Sorcha's entirely impure thoughts with an almost knowing smile upon his face, "I do have some ideas."

"Oh?"

"I was considering encouraging tourism around the loch – don't look at me like that, Sorcha."

How easily Murdoch slipped into using her first name, as he had done the evening before. Sorcha could not say she disliked it.

"What kind of tourism are you proposing, then?" she asked.

"Boating. Ferry rides. Controlled tours that mean large groups of tourists are never left alone to cause any harm to the countryside – accidental or otherwise. The loch is large and beautiful; there is plenty of space to indulge tourists upon it without disrupting local life."

Sorcha frowned, thinking of the kelpie. "And you... you do not worry for the tourists?"

"And why would I *worry* for them?"

"They might become distracted," she said, more to herself than to Murdoch. "They might get dragged beneath the surface of the loch. They might –"

Murdoch's laugh cut across Sorcha's concerns. "Are you referring to the kelpie? The one in your book?"

She nodded, though his laugh made Sorcha feel altogether rather silly for voicing her worries.

"I must profess to having lived in London far too long to believe such fairy stories," Murdoch said. He watched the sun burning low in the sky, a thoughtful expression on his face. "As a child things were different. Whenever I swam in the loch I'd imagine a black horse standing on the very surface of the water, encouraging me to get further and further from the shore until I was too tired to swim back. But that's all it was: my imagination. Such things as kelpies are not real."

Sorcha was silent, for she knew perfectly well that Murdoch was wrong. But she could not blame him for not believing in the kelpie – he truly had spent too long away from home, surrounded by those who would laugh at him in much the same way he'd laughed at Sorcha for thinking such things as faeries and water horses were real.

The two of them did not speak for a while, the quiet stretching out around them like the long shadows caused by the setting sun. Not too far in front of them a small part of the loch diverted into the forest, narrowing as if it were a burn. Sorcha knew it expanded again to form a pool not too far off the path through the trees. A small waterfall crashed into it; she used to disappear there on adventures with her childhood friends, daring one another to leap from the top of the waterfall into the dark, glassy water below.

And then Sorcha had an idea.

Lachlan said we need to make the kelpie show itself. That we need to get it away from the depths of the loch. So wouldn't an offshoot of it nestled in the forest be the perfect location to try and make him appear? The pool is barely twice my height deep.

"There is – there is somewhere I'd like to go before we head back to my parents, Mr Buchanan," Sorcha said, breaking the silence between them. "It's –"

"Are you referring to the waterfall pool?" he asked, leading Galileo down a path that crossed through the forest. "I must confess I was considering visiting it, too. My parents and I used to go on long walks simply to see it. I imagine it is beautiful at twilight."

Sorcha found herself smiling at the man in response. *Perhaps Murdoch is not such a lost cause. He might not believe in faeries anymore but his love for the land upon which he grew up is as genuine as my own.*

Murdoch lit a lantern to help guide them through the darkening forest. The trees glimmered around the edges with the last vestiges of the sun, as if they were lined with liquid gold. The air was filled with the songs of larks and wrens and warblers alike – a sign they were preparing to retire for the evening.

"Perhaps we should camp here for the night," Murdoch suggested when they were forced to stray from the forest path in order to follow the water. "It would be dangerous footing for Galileo to travel through the forest when it is truly dark."

Sorcha could hardly believe her luck, for now she would not have to beg Murdoch to delay travelling home for a final evening. She nodded enthusiastically. "I would like that very much."

A soft breeze rippled through the autumn-yellow ash and hazel trees that circled the clearing when they finally reached it, bringing with it the echoes of tawny owls hunting out of sight. Sorcha leapt down from Galileo, brushing down her dress and inhaling deeply to soak in the achingly familiar smells of ferns and moss and, though it was very faint, wild garlic.

Murdoch tied Galileo's reins to a hazel tree and joined Sorcha by the edge of the impossibly reflective pool, just as the sun set for good. Its dying rays turned the waterfall to liquid fire for but a second, and transformed the damp slate and granite surrounding the water's edge to glittering quartz.

In that one, dazzling moment of sunlight, Sorcha found herself watching Murdoch's face instead of the spectacle in front of her, looking for a sign. A sign that, deep inside his soul, he knew such places were full to the brim with magic. A sign that his faithlessness in things he could not see was a lie.

Instead all Sorcha witnessed was a now familiar, unknowable expression upon Murdoch's face, his dark eyes seemingly impervious to the lustrous sight before him. Sorcha was stricken with an overwhelming desire to take a step away from the man in fear...or a step forwards, instead.

That Sorcha did not know what she would do thrilled and unsettled her to no end.

CHAPTER TWENTY-ONE

Lachlan

There was something about Mr Buchanan – Murdoch – that Lachlan misliked a great deal. Perhaps it was because he was to be married to Clara, or that his predominantly London accent grated on Lachlan's ears, or that he'd prodded Lachlan with a stick until he'd been forced to run off.

Perhaps it was because Clara did not seem to hate the man at all.

Lachlan had watched the pair of them all day from a safe distance, taking note of the way Murdoch's eyes never strayed from Clara for very long. He saw the hunger in his gaze that Clara had professed to being scared of; Lachlan could not blame her. Murdoch was doubtlessly intimidating, so why did Clara continue to steal glances of her so-called betrothed behind locks of hair with cheeks rosy as apples?

She does not truly like him, Lachlan told himself over and over again as the sun crossed the sky and dipped low on the horizon. *For every lingering glance she just as equally flinches away from him. Mister Buchanan is a mystery to her.*

He didn't like that a mere human was more mysterious to Clara than the Prince of Faeries. Imprisoned as he was in his damned fox body Lachlan felt entirely inferior to the dark-haired man.

And now that man had entered the forest. *Lachlan's* forest. He hated it with every fibre of his being. *Just what is Clara thinking, going into the forest?* Lachlan wondered, frustrated and confused. *You are supposed to be on the look-out for the kelpie, or heading home so that I can steal you away through your bedroom window once everyone else is asleep.*

But then Lachlan heard the rush of water and realised exactly what Clara was thinking. "Clever girl," he murmured, thoroughly impressed by her idea as he followed the sound. The small waterfall pool Clara had stopped by connected an uphill burn to the loch, and was a perfect location to force the kelpie to show itself. Lachlan had no doubt that it would appear.

It wanted Clara, after all.

Lachlan was sure it did, otherwise it would have eaten her the moment she answered its call. Lachlan still couldn't bring himself to think of the kelpie as a 'he', despite Clara's previous insistence. It was hard enough dealing with Murdoch and Lachlan's own disgusting sense of jealousy towards the man; he did not need another male to contend with.

He watched as Clara finished pitching her tent far enough away from the pool to avoid getting splashed by the waterfall. Murdoch hung several lanterns around the clearing, casting a warm, flickering glow over everything.

Lachlan kept low to the ground, hiding in the shadows to avoid being seen; he did not want Murdoch to spot him and chase him away. But Lachlan knew he could not risk putting Clara to sleep, either, especially not after the way her dream had been interrupted the night before.

He had to find a way to talk to Clara as a fox.

And then he heard Clara say, "There are apple trees very close by, if I remember correctly. I might search for them whilst you tend to the fire, Mr Buchanan." Lachlan could not have thought of a more perfect reason for Clara to wander off on her own. From his hiding place he grinned at her with all of his sharp, gleaming teeth.

Murdoch stared long and hard at Clara as if he was sure she was up to something, then slowly nodded. "Do not stray too far, and do not take too long."

Clara flashed him a smile before picking up one of the lanterns and heading west through the forest. Lachlan followed on silent feet, waiting until she stopped and raised the lantern into the boughs of a tree to check for apples to make himself known.

"Clara," he hissed, darting forward to snake between her ankles and brush his tail against her legs. She bent her head to watch him with wide eyes, surprised but clearly delighted.

"I had hoped you were nearby," she said. When Lachlan jumped up onto his hind paws Clara lowered herself to the ground, putting down her lantern before scooping Lachlan into her arms. She squeezed him tightly, burying her nose into his fur. "I missed my fox prince."

A noise of disgust left Lachlan's throat. "Do not call

me that. It's insulting." Clara responded by kissing his head and running her fingers through his ruff. Lachlan thoroughly enjoyed the attention, and it left him feeling decidedly superior to Murdoch Buchanan. Clara had no qualms or fears about touching *him* the way she did her betrothed. She never flinched away from his touch, regardless of whether Lachlan was a fox or truly himself.

"But foxes are clever, cunning and handsome," Clara said, countering his protest with a small smile. "Are you saying it is insulting for me to associate such traits with you, Lachlan?"

"Very funny. I'm assuming you came through here for the pool."

Clara nodded. She tickled Lachlan's ears until he licked her chin. "You said we needed the kelpie to physically appear in front of us, so I figured this was the best way to do that."

"I agree. But what about your future husband? He is here, too."

Clara said nothing. She stroked Lachlan absent-mindedly for a while, which he revelled in. Then she sighed. "For better or worse Mr Buchanan will be witness to what happens. There is nothing that can be done."

Lachlan nipped her earlobe. "We could wait until tomorrow. You could allow the man to return you to your parents' house and then travel back here with me in the dead of night."

"But we are already here, Lachlan," Clara protested. Her eyes were bright with infectious excitement. "And you do not know how much you have. Better tonight than to delay."

162

Clara's words brought Lachlan starkly back to earth. He *was* running out of time, and with every day he left himself open to the possibility that he might be shot or trapped or otherwise injured, and then he'd lose himself forever.

He nodded. "You must make sure your Mr Buchanan does not interfere, then. Can you do that?"

She laughed. "I doubt he'd come swimming with me. You didn't, after all."

"I would have, had I not been a fox."

"Is that so?" Clara raised an eyebrow as if she did not believe Lachlan, though the fact that he'd said it meant it had to be true. Then she shook her head, laughing softly as she placed Lachlan down upon the forest floor and stood back up. She brushed stray strands of fur from her dress; in the lantern light they burned gold and orange and mahogany against the dark greens and blacks of the undergrowth. "I had best head back before Mr Buchanan grows suspicious."

"And what of the apples you promised him?"

She smirked. "The apples around here fell weeks ago. Mister Buchanan would know this, if he hadn't spent so many years in London."

Lachlan couldn't help but chuckle. *If it wasn't for the fact I dislike Murdoch I'd almost feel sorry for the man,* he thought, after Clara gave his ears a final stroke and rushed back towards the pool. Lachlan followed behind her at a much slower pace, hiding in a nook between two moss-covered rocks once he was close enough to the water's edge to keep a constant eye on Clara. Spray from the waterfall occasionally pattered against his head, but he didn't care.

"I think I was too late for the apples," he heard Clara inform Murdoch, who was cutting garlic and onions into a pot sitting over a merrily crackling fire. "Which is a shame. Apples from around here are delicious."

"A shame indeed," the man said. "Come by the fire and sit with me whilst I cook, Miss Darrow. It will be cold soon."

Clara looked at him strangely, then; Lachlan could not work out why. Then she gestured towards the pool with a flick of her wrist. "I thought I might...go for a swim, first. Care to join me?"

Murdoch laughed in disbelief. "You wish to swim? Now? The sun has gone down already!"

When Clara smiled at him it was devilish and enticing. Lachlan wondered if Clara knew how the man had been looking at her all day and was manipulating his feelings to her advantage, or whether she was simply like this all the time. *Both are as dangerous as each other, I suppose. She acts more like a faerie than a human.*

"I love swimming in the dark," she said, slyly unfastening her dress and allowing it fall to her feet. When she bent down to remove her stockings Lachlan was torn between watching Clara and watching Murdoch's reaction. He seemed stunned by her brazen attitude, though he did precisely nothing to stop Clara from slipping out of her chemise and letting it whisper past her skin to the ground.

Clara ran a hand through her hair, pulling it away from her face and shoulders to flow down her back. *She must know what she is doing,* Lachlan decided, unabashedly staring at the impossibly lovely, naked human before him. *She must.* A delighted shiver ran down Clara's spine when she dipped her toes in the –

presumably freezing – water. And then, with a final glance over her shoulder at Murdoch, she abandoned all caution and dived straight into the pool.

Jealousy stirred inside Lachlan when he looked at Murdoch. The man's eyes never left the pool as he waited for Clara to resurface, expression intent and dangerous to behold. His hands shook slightly at his side. Lachlan grew certain that if the kelpie did not appear tonight then the man would likely take Clara's bold actions as permission to lay his hands on her, and she could not possibly hope to fight him off.

He is bigger than me, Lachlan realised, then choked back a bitter laugh. Most anything was bigger than he was right now. But, at least, in his real form, Lachlan would have had his magic to fight the man. It would be no contest; Murdoch Buchanan would fall to the ground before he could touch a single hair on Clara's head.

But Lachlan wasn't himself. He was a fox.

He never thought he'd hope for a dangerous, deadly kelpie to show up in front of him; for the creature to try and take away a human he so badly wanted in front of Lachlan's very eyes. But it was better than watching Murdoch ravish Clara all night when Lachlan could do nothing about it, despite the obvious, deadly risks the kelpie posed.

Well, he supposed, as the surface of the pool settled back into a dark mirror above Clara's head, *there's a first time for everything.*

CHAPTER TWENTY-TWO

Sorcha

Knowing that both Murdoch Buchanan, her potential future husband, and Lachlan, the Prince of the Seelie Court, were watching Sorcha as she stripped off her clothes and slid beneath the cool, glassy surface of the forest pool sent a not-entirely-uncomfortable shiver down her spine.

The air was electric with tension. It was thrilling. It was dangerous.

There is something dreadfully wrong with me. I should not relish such an atmosphere.

But Sorcha did whether she wanted to admit it or not. She was playing a risky, potentially deadly game with her own life as bait and, instead of fleeing in fear, she was embracing the gamble. After all, if Lachlan was to be believed it wasn't just him and Murdoch who wanted her for something.

The moment her toes touched the water's edge Sorcha felt the kelpie's presence. She should have been scared, considering he'd almost drowned her before. She *was* scared. Terrified. But some instinct bigger than herself pulled Sorcha into the pool, diving straight into the centre of the freezing water to meet her fate.

Sorcha knew the water was barely twice her height deep; in the darkness of night it felt deeper. She could barely see a thing – the moon was yet to creep over the clearing to provide any light with which Sorcha could get her bearings. She swam down until she touched the bottom of the pool, feeling smooth granite beneath her fingertips as she edged over to the pressure of the waterfall. When she felt it hit her head Sorcha swam further still until she was behind it, then rose to the surface for air.

From her hiding place she could see the diffuse shape of Murdoch through the waterfall; he was walking towards the pool. Dread filled Sorcha's stomach, though it was mixed with excitement. *He cannot come in. Not when the kelpie is...somewhere. It is too dangerous.* Sorcha realised that perhaps Lachlan had been right to suggest waiting until Sorcha was alone once more to face the kelpie. If a giant, monstrous water horse showed up she had no idea what Murdoch might try to do.

But part of her wanted him to see it. Sorcha wanted him to know such things existed.

Lachlan himself was nowhere to be seen, though Sorcha assumed he was hiding close enough to the pool to jump in when he was needed. *And what exactly will he do?* she wondered. *And what will I do? When the kelpie appears do I simply continue our conversation where we left it last time? Or do I ask him why he let me get so close to death? Do I –*

Sorcha's thoughts were ripped from her head as the

current dragged her back beneath the surface of the pool and through the waterfall. But there hadn't *been* a current in the pool before; it had been still. Above Sorcha's head the water's surface remained calm, so completely at odds with the turbulence around her that she knew, instinctively, that it was the kelpie keeping her down.

She swung her head around wildly. "Where are you?" she called out. "I want to – I want to see you!"

Something even darker than the black water pinned Sorcha to the bottom of the pool. "Is that so?" the low, melodic voice of the kelpie said. "Or is it your fox friend who wishes to see me?"

Just like before, Sorcha caught a flash of silver and the glint of the kelpie's eyes for the smallest of moments before it dissipated once more. She reached out a hand through the darkness, desperate to cling to something. "We both want to see you!" she insisted, bubbles streaming from her mouth. "You said last time that you could help Lachlan. Won't you help him?"

"And what of you?" the kelpie replied. "Why do *you* wish to see me?"

"Because I –"

Something blocked her mouth, snaking around her teeth and tongue and lips to prevent her from speaking. Sorcha jerked away in panic, though the kelpie followed her.

"Stop wasting your air," he insisted. "Inside the water I can hear your thoughts. I told you that before."

This feels strange, Sorcha thought. Her eyes kept track of the ebb and flow of black-on-black in front of her, trying to catch a single defining detail of the creature keeping her locked in place. *How are you substantial enough to hold me down but not be seen?*

He laughed. "The loch is my domain. I control it. Now answer my question."

Sorcha was growing dizzy. She looked past the darkness of the kelpie to catch the glimmer of the pool's surface. Lachlan would be growing concerned. *And Murdoch? What will he think?*

"You are worried for both of them," the kelpie said. "Are you not worried for yourself?"

I should be, Sorcha admitted, *but I am not. I do not know why.*

"It is the same reason you wish to see me."

And then she *did* see him. The long line of an impossibly large horse's head, outlined in the silver of its intricate bridle. Flaring nostrils. Sleek, shining, ink-black hair. The flow of his mane in the water, entangled with weeds and shells and tiny, ghost-white bones.

And his eyes, darker than anything Sorcha had ever seen, and deeper than the loch.

Sorcha brushed a hand against the kelpie's face. He closed his eyes, long lashes fluttering for a moment before opening them once more. "You would never hurt me," she said, ignoring the kelpie's previous warning about using up her air. "You would never, because I have always wanted to meet you. That was all I wanted."

He nudged his nose against her face, reminding Sorcha of when Galileo had done the very same thing to her. "I will help you," he said. "But first you must do something for me."

Anything, she thought, knowing it to be true. *I'll do anything.*

"Then you must sleep, Sorcha Margaret Darrow."

Sorcha saw just a hint of the kelpie's teeth. They were wicked and sharp – not at all like a horse's. But Sorcha was feeling too euphoric to think them sinister. Too enthralled.

Too enchanted.

Without another thought Sorcha fell asleep, drifting into a dream just as heady and dark as the water around her had been. There was someone waiting for her, though their silhouette was indistinct. When Sorcha blinked focus into her eyes she took in his golden skin and pointed ears and lustrous, bronze hair.

"Lachlan," she cried, surprised, as he closed the distance between them.

His sun-coloured eyes were shining; his lips curled into a disbelieving smile. "You did it, Clara," he said. "You saved me."

"I did?" she wondered aloud. "I –"

Lachlan cut off her sentence with his mouth upon hers. "No more talking," he murmured, biting her lip the way he'd done the very first time he'd kissed her. "No more talking." He tangled his hands through Sorcha's hair, kissing her ever more insistently as she slid his shirt from his shoulders with fingers turned clumsy with desperate longing.

Sorcha was lost to Lachlan the moment their bodies fell to the floor.

CHAPTER TWENTY-THREE

Lachlan

When Clara hadn't resurfaced two minutes after diving into the pool Lachlan was seconds away from jumping in himself. He'd have done so sooner if the presence of Murdoch Buchanan hadn't given him pause; the man moved from his cooking fire over to the water's edge a few moments after Clara entered the water, taking off his boots to dangle his feet in the pool, and then –

Nothing. Murdoch had done nothing. He'd stared into the depths of the water, which in truth wasn't very deep at all, and had done absolutely nothing when Clara did not break back through the surface.

Lachlan felt the presence of the kelpie – that cold, horrific shiver down his spine that kept him frozen to the spot – shortly after Clara disappeared into the pool. Now it was stronger than ever. It was somewhere. *Somewhere.* But Lachlan could not see it; the water was too dark for him to make out any shifting, insubstantial shapes.

The monster was supposed to show its true form. It was supposed to appear before Clara to take her away. Was that not what it wanted? Was I wrong?

But then, when Lachlan moved a single paw forwards to slide into the water and find out what exactly was going on, Murdoch removed his coat and leapt in. He wasn't gone for long; the pool barely had time to settle above his head before he resurfaced with Clara in tow. She was unconscious, eyes closed and head lolling against the man's shoulder.

The presence of the kelpie did not disappear.

Every hair on Lachlan's body stood on end. *Just what is happening?* Lachlan thought, terribly concerned as he watched the man named Murdoch deftly climb out of the pool and gently place Clara down near the tent. Her skin was moon-white and glistening in the flickering glow of the fire; too ethereal to possibly be human. But Clara *was* human, and that was why she was so fragile. So easily threatened and subdued.

Murdoch slid Clara's sodden hair away from her face. He loomed over her, pressing his body against her own as if to protect her from the forest and all the nightmares it might contain. He stroked her cheek, a fond smile playing across his lips. The expression was so stark in contrast to what was actually going on that Lachlan found it deeply sinister. *What is he doing to Clara?* he wondered, tail twitching as Murdoch closed his eyes and lowered his forehead to touch Clara's.

When he kissed her Lachlan let out a hiss before he could stop himself. The man froze for but a moment, entire frame turned rigid, before he relaxed once more and returned his attention to Clara as if he had not heard anything awry.

Lachlan paced around in his hiding spot, infuriatingly confused. *He knows he is not alone. Something isn't adding up. Why is he doing this when Clara is unconscious?*

But then Murdoch's hands roved across Clara's breasts and waist and hips, and Lachlan forgot all about the fact he was currently a fox who had no chance of overpowering the man. He bolted forwards, stopping mere feet away him.

"Get away from Clara," he barked, hoping that Murdoch would be sufficiently shocked by the existence of a talking fox that he would back away from Clara immediately.

He did not. Instead, Murdoch continued his slow and assured exploration of Clara's body, though his lips curled into a wicked grin against hers. Lachlan bristled, forcing himself to take another step forward. "I mean it," he said. "Get away from –"

"What did you call Sorcha?" Murdoch asked softly, breaking away from Clara's lips for just long enough to respond. "Clara? How clever of her."

Sorcha?

But Lachlan refused to be rattled by the man's confusing response, for he realised in that moment that he did not, in fact, have to overpower Murdoch Buchanan.

All he had to do was put him to sleep.

But even as Lachlan thought of him with all his might, Murdoch laughed. "You are pathetic to even try such a trick, faerie. I suggest you don't come any closer; you can do nothing against me."

Lachlan moved closer nonetheless. "What are you?

You are not human."

"I could have rowan berries in my pocket. It is easy to block your kind from a human's sleep if one knows how to do it."

"And yet I do not believe you possess them. What do you want with Clara?"

Slowly, Murdoch moved away from the unconscious woman and retrieved his coat. He placed it over her just as gently as he'd stroked her cheek whilst Lachlan, desperate to keep him away from her, finally reached Clara's side. He caught sight of her face for just a moment; a disturbingly contented expression was upon it. Her lips were swollen and parted invitingly, and though the rest of her skin was ghostly pale her cheeks were flushed and hot.

She has been enchanted. She is dreaming. She –

Quick as lightning, Murdoch pulled out a dagger from his coat, taking advantage of Lachlan's temporary distraction to thrust it straight into his stomach.

"You know, for a fox, you aren't very clever," he said, twisting the blade until Lachlan screamed. He swayed dangerously on the spot until, finally, the man removed the dagger and allowed Lachlan to collapse to the forest floor. "You should have known not to get so close. I even warned you not to."

The last thing he saw before his eyes lost the ability to focus was Murdoch's very being twisting and turning into something else. Someone else. *No,* Lachlan thought, as he uselessly tried to fight off unconsciousness brought about by the intense pain in his stomach. *It can't be.*

But it was. For before Lachlan stood a perfect,

sneering imitation of himself, still shimmering around the edges, with a silver chain adorning his neck. It reflected the moonlight like a thousand tiny mirrors.

"Sleep peacefully, prince," the kelpie said, "for with an injury like that you will soon be naught but a fox."

By the time his doppelganger finished speaking Lachlan could no longer keep his eyes open. His muscles and then his brain grew heavy, smothering his blind panic for himself – and for Clara – until there was nothing left but darkness.

CHAPTER TWENTY-FOUR

Sorcha

"...to get up. Clara? Clara, you have been asleep for hours and hours!"

Sorcha's vision was hazy as she slowly blinked her way back into consciousness. Sunlight filtered down through the trees above them, informing her that it was almost noon. Sorcha had indeed slept for a long, long time.

Why did I sleep so heavily? I swam in the pool and –

Sorcha bolted upright so quickly that her head began to spin, but when she raised a hand to her forehead another hand beat her there. A golden hand.

Lachlan.

"Am I dreaming?!" Sorcha exclaimed, a wide smile growing across her face as she took in the appearance of the Prince of Faeries sitting beside her in the tent, not as a fox but very much as himself.

He matched her grin. "If this is a dream would you wish to wake from it?"

She shook her head, then noticed something shining around Lachlan's neck. An impossibly delicate, beautiful silver chain, just as stark against the faerie's golden skin as his mother's earring had been. Sorcha instinctively reached out a hand; Lachlan closed the distance between them until she could grasp it. She rubbed the metal between her fingertips, startled by the icy-cold surface of the tiny links that it was constructed from.

"Courtesy of the kelpie," Lachlan said. He tucked a lock of Sorcha's hair behind her ear, cocking his head to one side to look at her with curious, golden eyes. "What did you do to convince him to help us? I must admit I didn't believe it would be so easy."

"I...I do not know," Sorcha admitted. She frowned, trying hard to remember the night before. But then memories of her dream came rushing back and she recoiled from Lachlan, blushing furiously. "We –"

He chuckled at her response. "We did. You are not embarrassed, are you? We have so very nearly lain together in your dreams before, after all."

Sorcha's cheeks only grew ever more crimson. She crawled out of the tent and stumbled to her feet, realising in the process that someone had dressed her. "Did you –"

Lachlan chuckled as he exited behind her. "A gentleman cannot allow a young lady to sleep naked in a forest."

"And yet you left me to sleep naked by the loch-side three days ago."

"That was then. I'm a changed faerie."

Sorcha rolled her eyes, though she supposed Lachlan *had* changed since she first met him, even if only a little. She glanced at the kelpie's silver chain once more. "Were there...did the kelpie set conditions for your use of his bridle?"

"Yes," Lachlan said. "That much was expected. It must be returned after I've broken my stepfamily's curse, of course. He said you would know when he wanted it back; I'm assuming he'll contact you somehow."

"You're calling the kelpie a 'he' now. You didn't before."

Lachlan stilled for a moment then shrugged. "I suppose the least I can do after he helped us is to show the creature some basic courtesy." He picked up a fallen branch from a nearby hazel tree, using it to sweep away the ashes from the fire Murdoch had started the night before.

Murdoch.

Sorcha dashed around wildly to look for a sign of the man or his horse. But there was nothing left of him, not even his belongings.

"If you are looking for your betrothed," Lachlan called from behind her, "he saw me transform from a fox to a faerie. I told him to go. He did not want to leave you, but I assured him you would be safe."

"And he...believed you?"

"I cannot lie, can I?"

"He does not believe in faeries. He would not believe that."

Lachlan could only laugh. It was like a bell, chasing

away Sorcha's doubts and fears with every ringing note. "I think that, after seeing a beast materialise from water and a fox turn into a faerie, the man would believe anything."

Sorcha said nothing. She felt distinctly sorry for Murdoch; at the very least she had wanted to explain everything to his face. If he returned to her parents' house then perhaps she still could.

But first Sorcha had to help Lachlan.

"So...what now?" she asked, before turning to the tent to begin deconstructing it. Lachlan put a hand over hers; Sorcha's heart leapt at his touch. *He said it would be different to feel him in real life. If this is how I react to him merely touching my hand then how on earth will I handle anything else?*

"Leave the tent," Lachlan said, smiling wickedly at Sorcha's painfully flustered expression. "Leave everything. You will not need anything where we are going."

"So we're –"

"Going to the faerie realm, yes. I think it only fair that you get to witness the destruction of my stepfamily after everything you've done to help me, Clara."

She nodded, not trusting her voice to reply. Sorcha's heart was throbbing for an entirely different reason now – could she truly watch Lachlan murder his stepfather and stepbrother? *They are at fault,* she reminded herself. *They usurped his crown. They cursed him. They made him flee.*

"...yes," Sorcha finally said, entwining her fingers with Lachlan's despite the inevitable burning in her cheeks it caused. "Let us free you from your curse.

179

Though, I must profess, I was growing rather fond of you as a fox."

Lachlan kissed her hand, molten eyes locked on hers. "Something tells me I can make you far fonder of the real me."

"I very much look forward to it," Sorcha laughed softly, lips twisting into a smile that belied how sickeningly nervous she was. "But first..."

He grinned vindictively. "Yes: but first. First I have some Unseelie blood to spill."

CHAPTER TWENTY-FIVE

Lachlan

When Lachlan began to stir he felt inclined to fall straight back to sleep again. But then a stabbing pain in his stomach woke him with a start, and he yowled.

The kelpie. The kelpie. The kelpie was pretending to be Clara's betrothed, and now he is pretending to be me.

Lachlan didn't know what to do. He was in so much pain that he could barely move. But he *had* to; he had to reach the central faerie realm and foil the kelpie's nefarious plan before it was too late. Yet that thought gave Lachlan pause. "What *is* his plan?" he panted through gritted teeth. "Just what is he hoping to achieve by being me?"

It took everything Lachlan had inside him to struggle to his feet only to collapse to the ground once more. The pain from his stomach was blinding. *How can I move like this? How can I do anything at all?* He twisted his head around to look at the wound Murdoch – the kelpie – had inflicted. It wasn't enough to kill Lachlan if he kept it clean; it had been meant purely to slow him down.

"He said...he said I will soon be only a fox," Lachlan cried. "He wishes for me to suffer."

But if the kelpie wanted him to suffer then what did that mean for the rest of the Court? He had known Lachlan was a faerie – did he know exactly *which* faerie?

"Clara," he muttered. "He must have learned who I was from Clara. Which means..."

The kelpie knew everything he needed to know. He knew about Innis and Fergus, and of their plot to take over the throne. He knew they had tried to get rid of Lachlan. *But to what end is this information valuable to a creature of the loch? What does Murdoch want pretending to be me?*

It was hard not to think of the kelpie as 'Murdoch', though Lachlan knew it was a guise. But the kelpie had clearly been using the man's form for a few days, at the very least. He wondered when Murdoch Buchanan had ceased being himself.

Did Clara ever meet the real man? Did the kelpie drown him in the loch whilst he searched for her? Or had Murdoch been the monster from the beginning?

Lachlan's very bones turned to ice merely thinking about the kelpie inside Clara's house. "She told me he terrified her," he whispered, "and he did. He did. He was not a man. Not since she met him. I have to get up."

As a faerie Lachlan rarely spoke to himself out loud; as a fox he started doing so to ensure he was still 'himself'. Now, with the aching wound in his stomach, he needed to keep talking all the more, though words were difficult for him to wrap his sharp teeth and lolling tongue around. They sat thick in his throat. Foreign. Uncomfortable.

I am losing my speech.

It was this realisation that forced Lachlan back onto his feet, though he shook and whined and trembled as he did so. But he stayed up; though it took every ounce of concentration and strength of will Lachlan remained upright. He took an experimental step forwards and, though he flinched at how painful it was, Lachlan pushed through and took another. Another. Before he knew it Lachlan had made his way back to the waterfall pool where Clara's tent lay, unsurprisingly, abandoned.

He sniffed the canvas, revelling in her scent. She would be with the kelpie, Lachlan knew. After what he'd witnessed the night before he was sure the creature would not let Clara out of his sight.

He laughed at her name, Lachlan recalled. *He said she was clever. It was a false name all along.*

Her name is Sorcha.

Lachlan was deeply saddened by the knowledge that the kelpie had known Clara's real name when he had not. For he'd been able to enchant her, that much of which Lachlan was certain. For all he knew she was *still* enchanted, being forced to follow the kelpie against her will.

No, he thought. *Clara believes the kelpie is me. She is following the Prince of Faeries.*

That made Lachlan feel even worse.

Turning from the tent, Lachlan forced his feet to exit the clearing and begin the long, winding journey to the centre of the forest and the faerie realm. His stepfamily would be too threatened by the appearance of 'Lachlan' to realise that the real faerie prince was sneaking back in, still under the guise of a fox. He could get help. He *had* to get help – before it was too late for him to ask for it.

It took hours and hours for Lachlan to even reach the halfway point to the edge of the faerie realm. The pain in his stomach was excruciating; at this rate he wondered how he would ever make it. But then he picked up the scent of a faerie, and Lachlan stopped in his tracks. He sniffed the air to make sure he had not imagined the smell. It was coming from his right, towards the fringe of the forest where Lachlan had first met Clara.

On instinct he swung around and followed his nose, tail twitching in nervous excitement as the smell of the faerie grew stronger and stronger. *Someone,* Lachlan thought, darting through the trees as fast as he could physically bear to. *Anyone. Just one creature willing to –*

Lachlan froze. A tall, pale faerie waltzed through the twilit forest right in front of Lachlan's eyes, dressed in a sweeping, gauzy dress of periwinkle blue. Her ice-blonde hair flowed long and lustrous over her shoulders, never tangling or falling out of place. Her sapphire eyes were deeply, familiarly sad.

Ailith. It is Ailith.

If Lachlan had been in his original body he would have sobbed in relief; of all the faeries to run into he found the one who would help him no matter what. Without thinking he ran towards her, then yowled at the resultant stab of pain that clawed at his insides.

Ailith turned towards the noise, a frown shadowing her lovely eyes. When she spotted Lachlan she gasped.

"That is some wound, poor fox."

Lachlan opened his mouth to speak. But the words wouldn't come out; they stuck in his throat until he swallowed them back. He yipped and barked instead whilst every hair on his body stood on end.

"I shall leave you to get some rest," Ailith said soothingly. She backed away from Lachlan's display of aggression and fear, for she did not know he was angry and scared of himself, not her. But try as he might Lachlan could not force his body to follow the faerie; it resolutely did not want to.

No, no, no, no, he cried. *This can't be happening now, of all times.*

With a final sympathetic glance at him Ailith rushed off, walking too quickly for Lachlan to possibly keep up. He collapsed to the forest floor, exhausted beyond belief.

I have failed. I am going to be a fox for the rest of my life, and then I will die.

It was only then that Lachlan fully understood what the old faerie-fox had said before he'd passed away. His bullet wound was going to turn him into a fox forever, but it would kill him first. He was glad of it, for it meant he was still himself when he died.

Because of the cruelty of the kelpie Lachlan would not be granted that same small, blessed mercy.

He would die a fox, and nobody – not even Clara – would ever know.

CHAPTER TWENTY-SIX

Sorcha

Lachlan took hours leading Sorcha to the faerie realm. The sun had almost set by the time they drew close to the border, though Sorcha was glad of the longer journey; after everything that had happened thus far her nerves were decidedly frayed. Now they'd crossed over into the Seelie Court Sorcha's insides were roiling and leaping like Loch Lomond during a bad storm.

She sensed they'd entered the faerie realm before she saw any physical evidence of the change of location, for at first the realm itself looked no different from the forest surrounding it. Coniferous trees grew dark and close together, filling the air with the sweet smell of pine and preventing Sorcha from seeing much else of her surroundings but murky-coloured, prickly branches.

But then the trees began to spread apart once more and they changed from pine to ash and oak and hazel. The very ground upon which Sorcha walked seemed to glitter and glow; when she looked down her eyes picked out tiny fragments of semi-precious gemstones of every colour imaginable compounded into the earth. Quartz. Tourmaline. Jade. Amethyst. Lapis Lazuli.

Lanterns made of warped, clouded glass swung from every branch Sorcha locked eyes on, lighting up the gemstones to form a haphazard path through the forest. "Wow," she mouthed, at a loss for anything else to say. Part of her did not want to venture further into the faerie realm, for it unsettled her greatly, but for Lachlan's sake Sorcha resolutely took tentative step after tentative step down the path.

The eerie, swirling flames from the lanterns surrounding them made her skin so pale that Sorcha appeared almost a ghost. In contrast Lachlan's golden skin seemed more pronounced – luminous and rich and exotic. The glowing gemstone path filled his eyes with endless colours so beautiful that Sorcha could hardly bear to look at him.

Lachlan weaved his fingers through Sorcha's and squeezed her hand. "Do not be intimidated. This place is designed to make otherworldly creatures look as strange and alluring as possible to mortal eyes. Seelies are vain to a fault."

She couldn't help but snicker at Lachlan's easy admission of his kind's flaws. And it *did* make her feel better, though Sorcha still felt decidedly insubstantial in the torn and muddied dress she'd worn for three days straight and with her wild, tangled hair tumbling over her shoulders. She was reasonably certain there may have even been a twig or two stuck in it. But then Lachlan led her around a corner and Sorcha forgot all about her appearance.

"*Wow,*" she said again, for in front of Sorcha was the strangest building she had ever seen. The walls were curved and expansive, with a burnished gold finish that shone in the last rays of the sun. The ceiling melted perfectly into them without a seam or crack in sight. The entire building twisted and turned through the trees like a snake instead of stone – a feat impossible for mere mortal architecture. Though it was only one floor high Sorcha had the sneaking suspicion that the building likely continued underground.

Directly in front of them was an intricately carved, massive set of oak doors, which stood ajar. She turned to Lachlan, mouth agape. "Is this the pal–"

"Prince Lachlan?"

Sorcha started at the sound of the voice. It was ragged and hoarse – not at all like Lachlan's – and when she located the source of the sound she gasped. The Seelie creature who had spoken was all scales and talons and a short, sharp beak, though they stood upright like a human and wore the garb of a soldier.

Lachlan nodded his head at them. "In the flesh, as it were. Tell me; where are Innis and my beloved stepbrother, Fergus?"

The Seelie hesitated; their beady eyes seemed nervous beyond reckoning. "They said you – we thought you were gone for good, my prince."

"A lie to be sure," Lachlan said, laughing at his comment, since of course faeries could not lie. "So where are they?"

"They're finalising the hunting grounds for the day after the coronation and should be back soon," the guard said. "Would you like to rest in your chambers whilst you wait?"

Lachlan nodded. "If you could lead the way. I must

admit to being wary of navigating the tunnels alone when my stepfamily are nowhere to be seen. Please arrange for someone to bring more appropriate clothing along for my lovely companion."

The birdlike creature did not comment on Lachlan's ominous first sentence, instead sparing Sorcha a glance for the first time. They recoiled at the sight of her, eyes wide with shock. "A human!"

"A human indeed," Lachlan said. "Now lead the way to my chambers, if you will."

Sorcha remained silent as they entered through the oak doors into the palace. The internal walls seemed to glow from within, lighting the labyrinthine corridors in impossibly soft, golden tones. There were tears in her eyes before Sorcha knew it; the place was achingly beautiful. Beside her Lachlan was equally as silent, his expression uncharacteristically serious.

He never let go of Sorcha's hand.

"I will have someone bring clothes for the lady immediately," their Seelie guide announced when they arrived in front of a heavy wooden door just as ornately carved as the palace entryway. They bowed deeply. "And I shall see to food and drink being brought along, too."

The creature walked off without waiting for a word of thanks from Lachlan or Sorcha, leaving them to push open the door into the prince's chamber. Sorcha's pulse accelerated until she was acutely aware of her blood flowing through her neck and wrists and temples.

Inside, Lachlan's bedroom was lushly furnished. The largest mirror Sorcha had ever seen took up almost the entirety of one wall, its frame gilded in bronze and carved into endless Celtic knots. A thick, forest green rug sat upon the polished hardwood floor in front of a gaping fireplace, with a mantelpiece which was similarly carved like the mirror. Gauzy, pale gold curtains hung from a four poster bed. They rippled faintly as if there was a breeze in the room, though the air was still.

Beside the bed was an ebony table with a silver jug upon it. Lachlan let go of Sorcha's hand, closed the door behind them and wandered over to look inside the vessel, but it was empty. "What I wouldn't give for some wine," he sighed, throwing open the curtains around the bed before collapsing onto its silken covers. He smiled at Sorcha. "Come join me."

The request would have been outrageous coming from anybody else. But from a lazily grinning faerie prince in his half-undone, fine white shirt it seemed normal. Natural. Sorcha walked over to stand in front of him, brazenly beginning to unfasten her dress as she did so. Lachlan watched her do so like a hawk anticipating its next meal, filling Sorcha with a red-hot desire all her own. Her breath caught in her throat. And then –

The heavy door behind her was thrown open. "Lachlan?!" cried a voice coloured with obvious disbelief. "How –"

Sorcha turned just as Lachlan sat up on the bed. His eyes narrowed at the figure by the door, but then he smiled entirely humourlessly. "Well, if it isn't my dear stepbrother."

The Unseelie was tall, broad-shouldered and as silver-skinned as Lachlan was gold. His pointed ears were longer and narrower than his stepbrother's, and they were adorned with a multitude of small, hooped earrings. Both his eyes and hair were murky, midnight blue, which shone oddly in the flickering light of

Lachlan's bedroom.

Fergus' mouth hung agape revealing gleaming, pointed teeth. As with the Seelie guard before he did not seem to notice Sorcha. His gaze was locked solely on Lachlan. "You cannot – you should not be here."

"And yet I am. Is there a problem with that?"

"Lachlan?"

Behind Fergus another two figures appeared. One was male, and was paler and taller than Fergus. His irises were turquoise in colour, which suggested to Sorcha that he must be Lachlan's half-Unseelie stepfather, Innis. But it was the other faerie she took most notice of, with the long, ice-blonde hair, angelic white dress and wide, blue eyes, for she was the one who had spoken.

Sorcha knew that the heartbreakingly beautiful faerie could only be Ailith. On her left ear was the silver cuff Lachlan had been wearing the first time Sorcha met him – the one Fergus had stolen from him as proof that Lachlan had left the palace, and Ailith, forever. Sorcha didn't have it in her to be jealous of the faerie, even when Ailith's eyes filled with tears and she rushed past Sorcha to cling to Lachlan.

"They said you were gone!" she cried. "That you had left! How could you leave without speaking a single word to me first? How could you?"

Lachlan's face was blank as he reciprocated Ailith's embrace. "It does not matter. I am back now."

"We were certain you were gone for good," Innis said, inclining his head politely towards Lachlan. "I will admit I believed you to be."

When Lachlan extricated himself from Ailith to stand upright Sorcha had to admit that it certainly looked as if Ailith's love for him was genuine, despite Lachlan's previous assertions that she might never have felt for him what he felt for her. The faerie could not tear her eyes away from him. "We must celebrate your return tomorrow night," she said, a bright smile on her face.

Innis nodded. "Of course. The realm will rejoice to know that Lachlan has returned to us." His tone was mild and reasonable; if Sorcha hadn't known any better then she would not have believed Innis had anything to do with the plot to dispatch of his late wife's son. It was his *own* son who struggled to maintain his composure, making it obvious that something was awry, though when Innis fired him a warning glance the enraged faerie closed his mouth and remained silent.

What is this? Sorcha wondered, casting her gaze over first Innis, then Fergus, then Ailith and Lachlan. *Are they not going to discuss what actually happened? Surely Lachlan would want Ailith to know what her future husband did to her old love?*

But nobody said a thing. The conversation moved onto planning the following evening's celebration, leaving Sorcha feeling decidedly isolated and left out. This was not a place in which she belonged. But just as she began to shift away from the group Lachlan reached out a hand for hers, a gentle smile playing across his lips. Sorcha took it, simply because she did not know what else to do. She wished the top of her dress was not halfway unfastened, though she could do nothing about the state of her clothing now.

It was only then that the other faeries seemed to realise that Sorcha was there at all. "Lachlan, who is your human companion?" Innis asked, eyeing her curiously.

Lachlan grinned and pulled Sorcha close. "Why,

this is the human who helped my find my way back home. I very much intend for her to stay by my side in the long years to come." Lachlan kissed her hand, golden eyes full of such genuine affection that Sorcha's heart rate rapidly increased in earnest, despite their current audience. "My dear family," he announced, "this is Sorcha Darrow."

Just as quickly as Sorcha's heart had quickened it froze between beats, stuck on that one word that had not once fallen from the faerie's lips before now. A cold sweat began to form along her spine.

I never told Lachlan my real name.

CHAPTER TWENTY-SEVEN

Lachlan

"Julian, are you sure this is -"

"I was sure I could sense one of the Fair Folk, Evie, and there he was. This must be the faerie."

"Will he be alright?"

"Do not worry. He's -"

Lachlan coughed and spluttered, scrabbling to his feet when he realised he had fallen unconscious once more. It was daylight, though the sun was hitting Lachlan oddly. When his eyes finally focused he realised he was standing on a blanket-covered bench inside a stable. A dirt-streaked window was responsible for the diffuse light entering the room.

The wizard and his golden-haired partner stood in front of Lachlan, both wearing frowns of concern. "Faerie?" Julian wondered aloud. "It *is* you, isn't it?"

Lachlan nodded, not trusting his voice - fearful that it was gone forever. But then he became aware of something. Or, rather, the absence of something.

The pain in his stomach was gone.

"What did you do?!" he exclaimed, barking in excitement when he realised he could talk once more. Lachlan turned on the spot, inspecting the location where Murdoch had stabbed him. The fur was no longer matted with blood; all traces of the wound had disappeared.

"I healed you," Julian said. He scratched his chin as he cast a critical gaze over Lachlan. "My healing abilities are serviceable, so you should be fine, but I would still recommend you spending a day or two off your –"

"I do not have a day or two!" Lachlan cut in, all his urgency from the previous day returning in one fell swoop. Now that he was healed and could run and talk once more he had to head to the Seelie Court as soon as possible. This time he could not fail.

Julian's companion – whom the wizard had referred to as Evie when Lachlan was stirring from his sleep – stroked Lachlan's head and tickled his ears. "You must eat something, at least. I don't imagine you've eaten since you were attacked. Who did this to you, anyway? Does it have something to do with what you told us before? The change in 'management'?"

"...somewhat," Lachlan replied, licking the woman's hand in appreciation when she placed a bowl of chicken in front of him. His jaws snapped at the meat hungrily; now that his stomach had healed it had the capacity to recognise that it was painfully empty. He glanced up at the pair of humans. "A kelpie is posing as me right now and has made its way to the Seelie Court."

Julian's eyes widened. "A *kelpie*? That is dangerous

indeed."

Evie frowned at him. "What is a kelpie?"

"A water horse. It draws people to the loch in which it lives and drowns them, consuming their flesh and blood when they can no longer escape. They can change their shape at will using their silver bridle."

"But that is horrific!"

Lachlan stared at Julian, thoroughly impressed. "You know a lot for a foreign wizard."

"I enjoy learning about all kinds of magic," the man replied, as if his far-reaching knowledge was nothing of consequence. "So what is it that you need to do? How do you vanquish a kelpie?"

"I shall work that out when I reach the faerie realm."

"That doesn't sound like much of a plan," Evie admitted. "What can you do as a fox?"

Lachlan finished off the chicken before he replied. He twitched his tail, impatient to be off now that he was healed and full. "The Court will be distracted by the false me. I can use said distraction to find someone who can help to break my curse."

"You know how to?"

He grinned at the beautiful, golden-haired woman, thinking of how it would feel to see Fergus' lifeless body laying on the ground. "Indeed I do. Now, if you may be so kind: where exactly are we?"

"Darach," Julian replied. "MacPherson farm."

Unbidden, Lachlan thought of Clara's tale from back in the tent – of a red-haired boy stealing away her first kiss when they were children. *I need to save her,* he realised. *I must save her from the kelpie and then save myself. I am the reason she became embroiled in all of this in the first place.*

Without another word Lachlan leapt off the table and headed for the open stable door. He paused when he reached it, nose twitching. It had rained in the night; he hoped the forest floor would not be too slippery. The last thing Lachlan needed was to fall in the mud and break a leg. *How fragile I am when I am not a faerie.*

"Wait!"

Lachlan turned; Julian held out a hand as if to stop him. "What is it?"

"You owe me a favour for saving you," the wizard said, smiling slightly. "I just thought it prudent to ensure you acknowledged this."

Lachlan chuckled. "If I live through this then, indeed, the future King of the Seelie Court will owe you a favour. Thank you, human."

The sound of Evie crying out in wonder at the revelation that Lachlan was royalty kept a smile plastered on his face all the way back to the forest. Lachlan decidedly did not look at Loch Lomond, though it was mere feet away on his left. It would cause him to think about the kelpie, after all, and Lachlan did not want to think about the creature until he was in a position to get rid of it.

Lachlan glanced up at the sky and realised it was already late afternoon. *By the time I reach the faerie realm it will be past twilight. Everybody will be awake and celebrating 'my' return, no doubt. The more distracted they are the better.*

He reached the dark, forbidding pine trees that grew on the barrier between the mortal and faerie world much faster than he could possibly have reached them the day before. Lachlan barely dared to breathe as he passed beneath their boughs; every hair on his body stood on end at the subtle change in atmosphere. The birdsong filling the air lowered in pitch and intensity. Even the soft breeze felt altered.

Out of the corner of his eye Lachlan spotted a flash of brilliant white – a lithe, well-muscled stag, complete with impressive sixteen-pronged antlers. It stared at him as if it knew exactly who Lachlan was and was unafraid. Then, in the space of a blink, the stag was gone, silent as a ghost upon the wind.

Does it know it is to be hunted the day after the coronation ceremony? Lachlan wondered. He decided that, if he miraculously managed to get both his body and his throne back, he would call off the hunt. He'd spent long enough as a fox to understand the fear of being hunted in one's very home.

Lachlan crept through the realm, reaching the curved walls of the palace just as a group of drunk, revelrous faeries passed by the front entrance, taking turns to swig from a wine skin as they went. But they did not go through the intricately-carved wooden front doors; they carried on walking through the trees.

The celebrations are outdoors, then, Lachlan decided, stalking the group as closely as he dared until they reached the wide, moonlit clearing where most Seelie festivities took place. The clearing was encircled by a shallow, winter-cold burn, which bubbled merrily over innumerable fragments of amethyst and obsidian. Lanterns and torches burning with orange and blue and green flames were strung from tree branches and tall, wooden posts, casting the clearing in strange, swirling colour.

Everywhere there was dancing and eating and music. All manner of Seelie creatures were thoroughly absorbed in the celebration, though it could not have begun more than half an hour ago. Some were clothed in fine, expensively-woven garments adorned with gold buttons and glass droplets and every gemstone one could imagine. Others were stark naked, their skin taking on the colour of the flames burning all around them.

The sight should have filled Lachlan with a sense of relief; it was a familiar, beloved scene, after all. Instead his hackles were raised and his heart beat painfully fast, for there upon the centre plinth sat his silvered stepfather, Innis, and his stepbrother, Fergus. Ailith was sitting beside the treacherous Unseelie that was her future husband, one hand on his shoulder, though her crystalline, haunting eyes were on someone else entirely.

Lachlan. Or, rather, the kelpie. He stood there, contented and relaxed as if he had always belonged within the faerie realm. One hand rested on the pommel of a narrow sword hanging lazily from his waist. His right arm was slung around Clara.

Clara.

Lachlan had never seen her so beautiful. Someone had woven her unruly hair around her head and decorated it with bluebells, magicked back into season for this sole purpose. A translucent, sea-green dress fell to her bare feet in large swathes of weightless material, though it was cinched in at her waist and was held up by delicate straps made of silver chains. Despite the outrageousness of the dress – by human standards – Clara seemed decidedly unperturbed by the revealing outfit, though Lachlan could not say he was surprised. She'd swum naked in front of him on more than one occasion, after all.

And in front of Murdoch, Lachlan added on as he watched the kelpie parade about in Lachlan's best finery. The turquoise tailcoat he'd chosen to wear complemented both his borrowed golden skin and Clara's entire ensemble so achingly perfectly that jealousy clawed its way through Lachlan's throat. But he pushed it away for now; he had to.

And then he noticed the distance Clara had put between herself and the kelpie. It was subtle, but it was there. Only Lachlan could have noticed it, though, for after the many hours he'd spent curled against Clara's chest as a fox there was no requirement for distance between the two of them at all. Which meant –

"She knows," Lachlan whispered, winding his way through the packed clearing to get a closer view of the plinth. "She knows something is awry."

"I am so happy you are all here today to celebrate my return!" the Lachlan that was not Lachlan called out suddenly, so unnaturally loudly that the real Lachlan flinched where he stood. A claw-footed faerie trampled on his tail; he bit back a yowl before stalking behind a tree for his own safety. Everyone hushed to listen to their prince, immediately enraptured.

Innis was smiling good-naturedly from his high-backed, wooden chair, for he was well-practised at hiding his emotions. Fergus, on the other hand, could barely suppress a scowl at the figure of Lachlan. His entire body seemed to be shaking, though Ailith ran her hand up and down his arm as if to calm him.

The false Lachlan continued, a wide grin plastered to his face, "I am sure you are all wondering where I disappeared off to. My loving stepfamily told you that I ran away in my grief over my mother's death. I am here to tell you that isn't true. Not at all."

The clearing erupted into mutterings of confusion, but then Lachlan raised a hand and they grew silent once more. "I was betrayed, you see. Usurped. It pains me even now to say it, for I struggle to believe it."

"Who would dare usurp the prince?" someone wondered aloud, not far from the real Lachlan.

"There was nobody else vying for the throne before good Queen Evanna's death, was there?" said another.

The kelpie slid his arm away from Clara's waist, bringing her hand up to his lips to kiss it before leaving her to walk across the plinth. She took half a step after him, face coloured with concern, then seemed to think better of doing so. *Get away from there,* Lachlan thought at her, wishing more than ever that he could simply knock Clara unconscious on the spot and warn her about what was going on.

And then, without another word, the false Lachlan unsheathed his sword and drove it straight through Innis' heart, all the while grinning with ferocious pleasure. The Unseelie faerie stared at him, mouth open wide in shock, though Lachlan could see from his expression that he'd expected such a thing to happen. For how could he not, the moment 'Lachlan' returned to reclaim his throne?

It was Fergus who was genuinely surprised. Fergus, in his superiority and arrogance, who clearly believed that Lachlan would never return. When the kelpie removed his sword from Innis' crumpled, lifeless body Lachlan saw that, through the blood that was staining the metal, the sword was black.

Iron. Of course. The kelpie knew what he was

doing. But why is he helping *me? Does he truly mean to live as me for the rest of his days?*

But Lachlan knew what the kelpie did not. He was not a wounded, nameless fox, which the wretched creature had intended him to be by now. Once Fergus was dealt with Lachlan would return to his original body, and then he could destroy the kelpie with his own two hands.

Fergus leapt to his feet to face his false stepbrother, ire dripping from every pore of his silvery body. The kelpie seemed unperturbed; he took his time wiping the blood of Fergus' father upon the dead faerie's shirt. Ailith tried to pull her betrothed away, though Fergus shrugged her off.

"Tell me you did not betray Lachlan!" she demanded, voice full of tears and disbelief. "Tell me you did not –"

"You know I cannot tell you that," Fergus said, sparing Ailith half a glance before turning back and –

The kelpie swung its sword and took the Unseelie's head clean off. There had been no warning. No indication or tic that the sword was directed at Fergus' head. The kelpie had moved too quickly – so quickly, in fact, that Lachlan barely knew what had happened until the act was complete. The headless body collapsed first to its knees then onto its side. Ailith looked on, pale, glassy-eyed and horrified.

Clara could not look at the dead faerie at all; she turned away and buried her head in her hands. Lachlan thought for a moment that she might be sick.

The crowd screamed and cried, though many of the reactions were the result of vicious, riotous joy. Their prince was exacting his clearly well-deserved revenge, after all, and he was not the only faerie in the court who had mistrusted their Unseelie brethren. But as Lachlan stared at the kelpie kicking Fergus' grotesque, bloody head off the plinth and into the crowd something inside him grew cold.

For the one who had cursed him was dead, and he was still a fox.

CHAPTER TWENTY-EIGHT

Sorcha

Sorcha couldn't look at the bleeding, twisted bodies of the Unseelie faeries lain to waste at Lachlan's hands. *No, not Lachlan's,* she realised, frozen by the thought. *He is someone else. Something else.* For she was certain Lachlan had never known her real name. But there was another who had – someone who had read her thoughts and whose silver chain the false Lachlan was wearing around his neck, hidden by a high-collared shirt.

The kelpie.

"You..." Sorcha began, the word barely audible over the noise of the crowd. She stared at the Lachlan who was not Lachlan, though he was too busy riling up his audience to realise she was talking to him. She caught Ailith's eye but the faerie didn't seem to see her. She had fallen to her knees in a pool of Fergus' blood, staining her beautiful dress a dark, painful red.

Sorcha did not know why she did what she did next, nor how she found the strength to do it. She rushed across the plinth – ignoring the lifeless body of Lachlan's stepfather as he sagged from his chair to the floor, ignoring the sickening churning of her stomach – and grabbed Ailith's arm. One warning glare from Sorcha was all Ailith needed to wordlessly follow her through the crowd; by the time they reached the edge of the clearing the two of them were running full-pelt away from the bloody revelry.

"What just happened?!" Ailith cried between shallow, staggered breaths. "Why did he kill them?" Tears ran down her cheeks, glittering in the moonlight as if they were made from crystal. *She is beautiful even when she is heartbroken,* Sorcha thought. *No wonder Lachlan loves her so.*

"They deserved it," Sorcha gasped. "They turned Lachlan into a fox." Her stomach was in blinding pain from running so fast and so far, though she dared not stop. Something heavy and dreadful inside her told Sorcha that she could not let the kelpie find her. She fired a glance at Ailith who was, in turn, staring at Sorcha in disbelief.

"But that – on the plinth. That was not Lachlan. I know it in my very soul."

Sorcha nodded. "That was a kelpie."

Ailith jolted to a halt, her grip surprisingly strong on Sorcha's arm as she forced her to stop alongside her. The faerie's eyes were wide and horrified. "A *kelpie*?"

"From Loch Lomond," Sorcha replied. She looked at the ground, kicking at a fallen pile of leaves and pine needles as she did so. She was uncomfortable discussing the past fortnight of her life with a relative stranger – with the one Lachlan loved, no less. But she had to, so she did. "Lachlan and I, we...we sought it out. We needed his help."

"How could a kelpie have helped –"

"His bridle would have given me my body back and thus allowed me to drive a sword through my stepfather, and stepbrother, and break the curse they put on me."

Sorcha thought her heart would stop. She gulped, fearing having to turn and face 'Lachlan'. But when she inched around she was met not with the kelpie.

It was the real Lachlan.

He was still a fox.

"Lachlan!" Sorcha cried, delighted, bending down to scoop him up into her arms. She held him tight. "Where have you been? What happened to you?"

He nipped Sorcha's ear. "The kelpie enchanted you and put you to sleep," he explained, "then he drove a dagger through my stomach. When I awoke the two of you were gone, and I tried desperately to find some help before my wound turned me into a fox for good."

Ailith dropped to her knees, ashen-faced. "You – I saw you yesterday. I saw you, and I walked away."

Lachlan slid out from Sorcha's grasp to sit in front of Ailith. He rested his front paws on her knees, though her dress was soaked through with dark, sticky blood. When she lowered her head Lachlan touched the tip of his twitching nose to hers. Ailith closed her eyes and let out a sob.

"You believed me a fox," Lachlan reassured her. He licked her cheek. "When I found you I *was* one, because of my injury. If it wasn't for Julian then I –"

"Julian?"

"A foreign wizard," he explained, glancing back at

Sorcha as he spoke. "I met him in the forest a sennight ago. He was searching for another faerie who had been turned into a fox four years ago."

Sorcha frowned. "That wouldn't have anything to do with your stepbrother cursing *you*, would it?"

"It was Innis who cursed the unfortunate creature. The faerie in question vocally protested the bloody Unseelie's marriage to my mother. Innis silenced him in the cruellest way imaginable. Clearly the son takes after the father."

Ailith let out a garbled cry. "Why did they do this, Lachlan? Why did they curse you? What were they hoping to achieve?"

"A question for another time," Sorcha cut in, realising in that very moment that there was a far more pressing matter to discuss. She brushed her fingers against Lachlan's tail. "Why are you still a fox, Lachlan? With Fergus' death your curse should have been lifted."

Even as a fox Lachlan looked obviously troubled. "I do not know. I don't understand what's going on. It makes no sense."

The three of them sat upon the forest floor in silence, both Sorcha and Ailith staring at the conundrum that was Lachlan, the fox prince. A cool, heady breeze passed through the trees, billowing Sorcha's insubstantial dress around her and causing Ailith's earring to chime like a bell.

No, not Ailith's earring, Sorcha realised, a flash of inspiration and certainty crossing through her brain in response to the sound. *Lachlan's.*

Without a warning to either of her companions Sorcha darted out her hand and wrenched the silver cuff from Ailith's ear, causing her to yelp in pain and surprise. Sorcha had no time to apologise; she held the beautiful, innocuous piece of jewellery up to the moonlight, looking for some kind of sign that it was more than it seemed. The tiny chains and minuscule sapphires that adorned it blew gently in the breeze, threatening to enchant Sorcha then and there by virtue of simply existing.

Then she threw it to the ground and unceremoniously smashed it over and over again with a rock, much to the shock and dismay of Ailith.

"What are you doing?! That was -"

"Cursed," Sorcha bit out, lips curling in bitter satisfaction as the chains were shorn from the earring and the beaten silver cuff began to warp beneath the weight of the rock. "We need to destroy it."

"Clara - Sorcha - you're a genius," Lachlan muttered. He stood up and turned to Ailith. "Ailith, it will take more than a rock to dismantle it. Could you do the honours?"

The faerie regarded him somewhat doubtfully but picked up the earring nonetheless when Sorcha obediently stopped trying to smash it into pieces. Ailith curled her hand around it, squeezing it tightly as if her body contained the strength to pulverise metal. Her pupils contracted and expanded, and she breathed in deeply through her nose, and when she opened her hand a few moments later the earring had been reduced to a tiny pile of glittering dust.

Sorcha gasped. "You are so strong!"

Ailith laughed softly. "Not strong in the physical sense. That was magic."

"And excellently done, as usual," Lachlan said. He leaned forward to blow the dust away, startling both Sorcha and Ailith in the process, for he was no longer a fox.

The curse had been broken, and neither of them had thought to watch Lachlan as they broke it.

He grinned at Sorcha, all perfect, white teeth and golden cheeks. "I can't believe I hadn't realised the earring held the curse. You are so clever."

"If I was clever I'd have thought of it *before* I dived into the loch and – oh. *Oh.*"

"What is it?" Lachlan asked when Sorcha did not elaborate. She stood up and walked over to a hazel tree, rubbing her fingertips across the bark as she lost herself to a deeply troubling thought. Ailith and Lachlan both stood up and followed her; Lachlan took Sorcha's hands in his own, a frown of concern colouring his expression. "What is wrong?"

"I was told that Mr Buchanan left after 'you' turned back into a faerie and made him go," she said, very, very quietly. "He had not wanted to leave me, but you convinced him otherwise. But it was not you that Murdoch was speaking to; it was the kelpie." Sorcha was shaking; she couldn't help it. She stared at Lachlan, hoping against hope that he could assuage her fears. "Lachlan, do you know what really happened to him? If he is dead because of me I couldn't –"

"Sorcha," Lachlan interrupted. His face was so grave Sorcha could hardly bear to keep her eyes on his, so she broke away from his touch as if he had burned her.

"No," she uttered. "He can't be dead. He can't –"

"Murdoch Buchanan *is* the kelpie."

CHAPTER TWENTY-NINE

Lachlan

"Cla-Sorcha," Lachlan began, "say something. Anything."

Sorcha's real name felt odd upon Lachlan's tongue as if it didn't belong there. But, in truth, it was the name she had given *him* that did not belong. Lachlan had to remember that. It had been a line of defence against him; given what the kelpie had done with her real name Lachlan fully understood why Sorcha had been so cautious.

"You are lying," Sorcha whispered. She ran her hands up and down her arms as if she was freezing. Considering how thin and wispy the material of her dress was she may well have been. With every gust of wind that blew through the trees a bluebell fell from her woven hair, which was itself beginning to come undone. It gave Sorcha the appearance of a girl whose enchantment had come to a stark and shocking end, which was not far from the truth at all.

"You know I cannot lie," Lachlan said, not unkindly. "Sorcha, Murdoch is the kelpie. He was masquerading as the man for as long as you knew him. I am so deeply sorry."

"Miss Sorcha, you – you knew the kelpie *personally?*" Ailith asked, incredulous. "How in the world..."

"He had taken on the form of the man she was engaged to marry," Lachlan explained, keeping his voice soft for Sorcha's benefit. She was staring at her bare feet; they were filthy from having fled so quickly through the forest. "He knew her full name."

Ailith's mouth formed an *o* of understanding. She turned a sympathetic eye to Sorcha. "This must be very hard for you to wrap your head around, Miss Sorcha. You –"

"I am fine," Sorcha cut in, clearly not fine at all. She looked at Lachlan. "We have to stop him. How?"

"Surely all we have to do is expose him as the imposter that he is," Ailith thought aloud.

But Lachlan shook his head. "And then what? We have no idea what it is that the kelpie actually wants. So long as he has the power to take on the form of anyone he pleases then he will be free to trick anyone and everyone time and time again."

"Then we take his bridle." Both Lachlan and Ailith stared at Sorcha. She smiled grimly. "We take the silver chain from his neck and keep it from him until the end of time. If he cannot change shape they he'll have no choice but to return to Loch Lomond."

"But how do we take the bridle from him?" Ailith asked. Lachlan scratched his chin as he pondered a solution but it was Sorcha who, once more, provided the answer.

"I will do it," she said, gazing past Lachlan in the direction of the palace. Her mismatched eyes seemed made of glass – emotionless and empty. He knew it was a front, so he closed the gap between them once more and encircled Sorcha in his arms.

"I will not have you do this," Lachlan murmured into her hair, breathing in the smell of bluebells and the faintest hint of lilac as he did so. He crushed her against his chest. "You can't face him alone. You can't."

"I can and I shall. I have to." Sorcha softly pushed Lachlan away to look up at him; her lips were set in a miserable, determined line. "I can take the chain from him when he's sleeping. It is our best option."

"The coronation ceremony is tomorrow," Lachlan countered. "We could do it then, when we have an audience to witness what happens. We would have support against the kelpie."

Sorcha nodded. "If I fail then we can do that. But as it stands my plan is safer...for everyone. Which means I must go now."

"You – no," Lachlan insisted. He squeezed Sorcha's forearms a little too tightly until she winced. "I don't want you to be alone with –"

"Lachlan, let her go," Ailith cut in, reaching forward and forcibly loosening his grip on Sorcha. "She is right. Let her do what needs to be done."

Sorcha inclined her head politely towards Ailith before shaking Lachlan off. "You will know if I have failed if you don't see me before the sun is up," she said, before turning to run back towards the palace like a

212

pale green, bare-footed ghost. Lachlan strode a few steps after her; a delicate hand on his wrist stopped him from getting very far.

"She will be fine," Ailith reassured him. "I trust her."

"You do? You do not know her at all."

"Yes, but you do, and she has done right by you so far. How could I *not* trust her?"

Lachlan sighed heavily and crumpled against a tree, sliding down to the forest floor to languish in amongst fallen pine needles and yellowed ash leaves. He almost wished he were a fox so that he could roll about in them. "This is madness, Ailith," he muttered. "Utter madness. Is this what being king will be like each and every day?"

Ailith gracefully folded her knees beneath her to kneel by Lachlan. "Why did Innis and Fergus try to remove you from the throne?" she asked, voice barely a whisper. The stench of Fergus' blood on her dress was so overwhelming that Lachlan had to fight the urge to recoil away from her.

He cocked his head to one side, frowning as he scratched his ear where his earring used to be. "They deemed me unfit to rule," he explained. "They were certain Fergus himself would do a far better job in my stead, with you by his side. To be honest I haven't yet discounted the idea that this was all a ploy to overthrow the Seelie Court."

"That...would be a serious problem, indeed," Ailith replied. She wiped away her remaining, unshed tears and sat up a little straighter. "There haven't been any problems between our races for decades, Lachlan. What makes you think this is a direct attack on us?"

"Because they are Unseelie, and we are not."

"That isn't a good enough reason, Lachlan! Innis loved your mother!"

"That may be so," Lachlan acknowledged. "I do not deny that he did, but that does not mean my theory isn't correct, either. But at least now I know why Fergus fought so hard for your hand."

Ailith hesitated. "And why is that?"

"Because everyone loves you. You would make a great queen. I would know, given the fact I wished to marry you myself."

"Lachlan –"

"Why did you agree to marry him, Ailith?" he interrupted, forcing Ailith to maintain eye contact with a sharp stare she had no power to turn away from. "I do not believe you loved him. So why did you break my heart to be with him?"

She was silent for a minute; to Lachlan it felt as if it stretched on for forever. But just as he was about to repeat his question Ailith sighed and shook her head. "Because your mother told me I could not be with you. She had foreseen who I would be with in the end – and it wasn't you. She did not want me to marry you only to break your heart when I inevitably left you for another in the future."

"And you *listened* to her?" Lachlan asked, incredulous. "You followed a premonition instead of the way you felt? Ailith, you know that Seelie visions have been wrong before! There are so many ways to interpret them. There –"

"You would have had me disobey a direct order from my queen?"

"That still does not explain why you agreed to marry *Fergus*," Lachlan countered, quietly furious. "How could you do that to me?"

"Fergus was good to me," Ailith said, eyes bright and shining with a fresh batch of tears. "I thought I could be happy with him, and I could at least be a sister to you. I –"

"I never wanted you to be my sister!"

In a rush of fumbled footsteps and ragged breaths Lachlan tore himself away from her, no longer able to sit beside the faerie who had broken his heart. But Ailith followed, clinging to his sleeve to force him to stop.

"Lachlan, I'm sorry," she said. He did not look at her. "You know I love you dearly. I believed I was doing what was best for the both of us. If I was wrong then so be it; I'm mature enough to admit it."

"He was the one who cursed me," he muttered. "Fergus, I mean. He laughed in my face, sneering that he was much better suited to the throne than I was, and doomed me to die as a fox. His father agreed that I wasn't ready to be king, too. And it wasn't a lie, for he could not have said it if it was." He glanced at Ailith; her expression was endlessly sad. "What do you think? Do you think I would make a useless king?"

"I think that, as long as you're open to listening to those who want the best for the realm – and for you – you will make a fine king, Lachlan."

"So if I asked you to rule by my side, you would agree?"

Ailith hesitated for a moment. "You want me to be

215

queen? After everything that's happened?"

"*Especially* after everything that's happened. Fergus had one thing completely right," Lachlan said, finally turning to face her. "You would make a wonderful queen. You are rational and fair, and you would ensure I do not destroy our relationship with the Unseelie on the basis of a grudge. The Court loves you. And I love you, though in what way I can no longer be sure."

Ailith cast her gaze over her shoulder towards the palace. "Is your change of heart related to Miss Sorcha?"

Lachlan said nothing, which spoke far louder than any words he might have uttered. Ailith smiled when she caught the hint of a blush spreading across his cheeks.

"I never thought I would see the day. Lachlan, Prince of Faeries, enchanted by a mortal girl."

"That's because she *is* enchanting. You should hear her sing, Ailith."

She took his hand. "Then I hope that, one day, I will. But for now I must keep you hidden and trust that Miss Sorcha will be successful tonight."

Lachlan shuddered. For everyone's sake he hoped she would be able to strip the kelpie of his silver chain and be done with it sooner rather than later. But he could not stand the thought of Sorcha being alone with the monster.

He knows her name. He could enchant her again.

Abruptly Lachlan did an about-turn and headed towards the palace. "Whatever are you doing, Lachlan?!" Ailith cried out in shock. "You will be seen!"

"I won't and you know it," he replied, grinning. "I am an expert at sneaking about, or have you forgotten? I cannot leave Sorcha without any protection. I shall keep watch from the shadows."

Ailith couldn't help but laugh into her hand at his certainty. "You truly are a fox."

If it meant he could keep Sorcha safe then Lachlan was happy to agree with her.

CHAPTER THIRTY

Sorcha

The golden palace corridors cast Sorcha's skin in a warm, ephemeral glow as she crept along to Lachlan's chambers. Given how many twists and turns there were she was surprised she remembered the way, but by resolutely following her instincts Sorcha found herself outside the heavy wooden door of his room before she knew it.

Let the kelpie still be at the revel, she begged. *Let me have some time alone to collect my thoughts.* For Sorcha had no idea how she was supposed to act as if she didn't know who the false Lachlan really was, and she was still reeling from the revelation that the kelpie had been posing as Murdoch Buchanan all along. If Lachlan was to be believed then Sorcha had never known the real Murdoch at all.

A shiver ran down her spine as she recalled all the time she'd spent alone with the kelpie, thinking him her potential future husband. *What would have happened if I never ran off to look for him with Lachlan? Would the kelpie have continued to pretend to be Murdoch? For what reason? What could a kelpie hope to gain by marrying a human?*

Sorcha had never been so conflicted and confused in all her life. But she couldn't stand there by the door, shaking and shivering and over-thinking everything to death, when she had a job to do. No matter what happened Sorcha had to steal the kelpie's bridle away. She *had* to. There was too much riding on her being successful to fail now.

And so, inhaling deeply, Sorcha turned a carved, bronze doorknob and eased her way into Lachlan's chambers. The door closed behind her on well-oiled hinges, barely making a sound as it clicked back into place. Sorcha surveyed her surroundings; the room was dark save for a fire burning merrily in the hearth casting long shadows across the floor. For a moment Sorcha was certain she was alone, so she let out her breath in one large gust of air.

"I was looking for you."

Sorcha jumped in fright, for Lachlan's voice echoed all around the room. But then she realised that it originated from the four poster bed; the gauzy curtains had been pulled shut, effectively obscuring the kelpie posing as Lachlan from view. But now that Sorcha was looking at the bed she could just barely make out a shape shifting behind the airy fabric.

She gulped. "I...was not prepared for what I saw today," she said, hating that her voice trembled. "I must confess to having run from it."

A golden hand pulled back one of the curtains. The false Lachlan swung his legs around to sit on the edge of the bed, eyes locked on Sorcha's every move. His hair was wavy and unbraided down his back as if he had only just brushed it through, and he had removed much of his bloodied clothing from earlier to leave only a pair of doe-skin breeches and the silver chain around his neck preserving his modesty. Sorcha found herself staring at him with increasingly rosy cheeks even though she knew it was not truly Lachlan.

When I lay with him in my dream, Sorcha realised with dismay, *it was not Lachlan, either. It was a fantasy woven by the kelpie. Does that mean –*

"I know you aren't Lachlan," Sorcha said before she could stop herself. But there was no way she could continue to lie, not when the faerie's eyes held an intensity Sorcha knew belonged in Murdoch's impossibly dark ones.

The kelpie did not respond for a second. Two. Sorcha hardly dared to breathe. And then, when she thought that her heart might burst through her chest from anticipation and fear, the kelpie dropped his faerie prince guise and returned to the form of Murdoch Buchanan.

"How did you know?" he asked, in a voice that Sorcha had been certain she would never hear again.

"My name," she whispered. "You used my real name yesterday. Lachlan never knew it."

The kelpie burst out laughing; Sorcha bristled away from it. "A foolish slip-up on my part. But it was so hard to keep calling you Clara, Miss Darrow. Come, sit with me."

"I –"

"If I was going to harm you I'd have done it by now. You must know that, given how many opportunities I had to do so over the past fortnight."

Sorcha hesitated for a moment. Then, on unsteady legs, she stumbled over to the bed and sat by the kelpie without once looking at him. When he brushed his hand against her hair and pulled out a bluebell Sorcha struggled not to flinch.

"Your hair is coming undone," he murmured, leaning in close to twist a lock of it back into place. "You looked so beautiful today. I could hardly take my eyes off you."

"What – what is it that you want from me, kelpie?" Sorcha stammered. She kept her eyes forward, still too fearful to look at him as he continued to fix her hair with gentle fingers. All she could think about was how those same fingers had so easily wrapped themselves around the hilt of a blackened, iron sword and driven it through the heart of a faerie.

And decapitated another.

The kelpie stroked the back of his hand along Sorcha's jaw. "You can call me Murdoch, if you want to. Or Mr Buchanan, if you prefer the formality. I've grown rather fond of the name."

Sorcha twisted around to face him, her desire to gather answers finally overcoming her fear of the creature. "You killed him. You *killed* him. When did you –"

"You never met the man," Murdoch explained. "Your father met him twice. On his third visit – before arriving at the Darrow household – Mr Buchanan took Galileo for a stroll along the loch shore. Suffice to say he never returned from his walk." He chuckled darkly. "He was an ambitious man, Sorcha. A good man, once, but

221

London changed him. And a Lothario if ever there was one. You would have quite rightfully run from him."

"But *why* did you pretend to be him?" she asked insistently. "What possible reason could you have to do such a thing? You did not know about Lachlan and his curse until I told you about it in the loch four days ago. So why did you do it?"

Murdoch stared at Sorcha as if she had lost her mind. He shook his head in disbelief. "I saw an opportunity to protect the loch and I took it. By taking on Mr Buchanan's appearance I could control any external influences trying to change the area. I'll admit, when I dragged him beneath the water and consumed his body and soul I had not expected him to be so useful."

He smiled at Sorcha, his dark eyes warm and happy for once. "And to think that he was to marry *you,* Sorcha. You, whom I had heard on countless occasions singing to the ducks and regaling the swans about your day cleaning up after bouts of particularly untidy tourists. I saw the way you watched the loch ebb and flow for hours, doing naught but thinking. Of course I wanted to meet you. Murdoch Buchanan was the perfect vessel through which to do so."

Sorcha was overwhelmed by Murdoch's explanation. It had not been what she expected in the slightest. *But what was I expecting, anyway? After all my previous encounters with the kelpie, in both the loch and as Murdoch, I'd have been lying to myself if I thought he meant me harm. But this means...*

Her face burned red-hot, so Sorcha turned away from Murdoch to hide the flush of her cheeks. But then, to her surprise, he dragged her down to lie upon the pillows with a hand on her shoulder, turning her back around to meet his eyes in the process.

"I do not need to be in the loch to read your thoughts with a face like this, Sorcha," Murdoch said, smiling softly. There was a glint in his eyes that Sorcha had seen on numerous, dangerous occasions – a glint that constantly had her torn between running away screaming and leaning in closer to surrender to it.

Murdoch ran the pad of his thumb over Sorcha's lips, smile widening into a grin when she gasped. "What are you doing?" she asked in a whisper. Sorcha became all too aware, in that moment, of how translucent her soft green dress was, and how easily Murdoch could slip its delicate, silvered chain straps off her shoulders.

The chain, she remembered with a start, eyes locking on the flashing metal around Murdoch's neck. It looked different on him than it had done on 'Lachlan'. It was like it belonged there – silver on moon-white skin instead of clashing with gold – though in truth the man's body was no more the kelpie's than Lachlan's had been.

Murdoch frowned when he noticed where Sorcha had diverted her attention. "What are *you* doing?" he asked. "Why are you looking at my bridle like that?"

Though Sorcha was flustered and Murdoch much too close, she steadied her heart and urged herself to ask the most important question of all. "Why are you pretending to be Lachlan? What do you hope to gain from it all? And where is – where is he?"

Sorcha added her final question when she realised that Murdoch did not know that she'd already seen Lachlan, and broken his curse, and that it would be strange for her not to ask after him.

Murdoch grimaced. "Do not think of him, Sorcha. He wished to enchant you into doing his bidding from the very moment he met you. He –"

"I already knew that," she cut in, "and yet you did the same thing. You enchanted me into thinking I was with him. You are no better than he is."

"I...deserve that," Murdoch relented, though every muscle in his body had grown tense. "But I had to do it. I could not pass up an opportunity to infiltrate the Seelie Court."

"But *why*?"

"...you will see. Tomorrow. I do not wish to talk about faeries and their vile, parasitic ways right now."

"So where is –"

"Gone," he spat. "A fox for good. I could have killed him, but I didn't. I knew you would never forgive me if I did."

"And you thought I would be willing to forgive you for dooming him to lose himself, instead?"

Murdoch sighed. He stroked Sorcha's cheek somewhat absent-mindedly. "You had hardly known him for any time at all, Sorcha. I have known you your entire life. You will get over this."

She stilled beneath his fingers, struggling to comprehend such an idea as the kelpie having known of her existence for twenty years. She wondered how immeasurably old he was, but could not bring herself to ask him.

And then Murdoch rolled onto his back and closed his eyes. "Won't you sing for me?" he asked, the question so quiet it was barely audible. "The way you always did before, when you could not see me listening from the loch."

Sorcha found herself watching Murdoch for a long, drawn-out minute without responding. She took note of the planes of his pale, angular face; his black hair curling around his ears and falling across his forehead; his broad shoulders and well-defined chest; the way he drew in his stomach when he breathed.

"Keep looking at me like that at your own risk, Sorcha," Murdoch murmured without opening his eyes. She sat up immediately, mortified. She hated how painful the throbbing of her heart was against her ribcage, and how her mind had gone racing back to the night when Murdoch had held her close and kissed her neck.

"O thou pale orb that silent shines," Sorcha began, desperate to rid herself of any and all dangerous thoughts and desires. Her voice was quavery and insubstantial at first, so she coughed to clear her throat before continuing.

"While care-untroubled mortals sleep!

Thou seest a wretch who inly pines.

And wanders here to wail and weep!

With woe I nightly vigils keep,

Beneath thy wan, unwarming beam;

And mourn, in lamentation deep,

How life and love are all a dream!"

Sorcha sang and sang her way through the long, impossibly relevant poem, watching the smallest of smiles curl Murdoch's lips as his breathing grew ever more relaxed. She had never witnessed him so calm and

225

free before. The feeling of singing to him was achingly nostalgic, as if she truly was sitting upon the loch-side watching the sun set across the water.

When she reached the final verse of her song Sorcha realised that she was sad it was coming to an end; it felt like no time had passed at all. She had hoped the seconds would somehow stretch out into eternity.

"Oh! scenes in strong remembrance set!

Scenes, never, never to return!

Scenes, if in stupor I forget,

Again I feel, again I burn!

From ev'ry joy and pleasure torn,

Life's weary vale I'll wander thro';

And hopeless, comfortless, I'll mourn

A faithless woman's broken vow!"

The silence that followed Sorcha's final note was tense and tragic. She realised she was waiting for a reaction from Murdoch. A smile, perhaps. For him to open his eyes and stare into her very soul. Part of her wanted Murdoch to reach out a hand and grab her – to pull Sorcha beneath him and crush his mouth to hers with desperate, intense longing.

But Murdoch had fallen asleep.

CHAPTER THIRTY-ONE

Lachlan

She sang for him. The kelpie. Why did she sing for him?

Lachlan reached the door to his chambers just after Sorcha herself entered the room. He hadn't been able to stand the idea of leaving her alone with the kelpie – not after witnessing the way the creature had looked at her through Murdoch Buchanan's eyes. Now his suspicions were confirmed.

I was right to believe he wanted her from the very beginning. And now I know why. The damn thing is in love with her.

He never thought he'd see the day a kelpie fell prey to such emotions.

The final straw was when Sorcha's melodic, haunting voice began to filter through the door. Lachlan was beyond jealous; he hated feeling this way. He was supposed to be above such emotions. Beyond it. But when the silence stretched out for far longer than he expected once Sorcha finished her song Lachlan began to grow suspicious. *Just what is going on?*

He was seconds away from cracking open the door to see what was going on when Sorcha herself opened it, a thin sliver of firelight creeping through to filter across the corridor. Her blue-and-green eyes caught sight of Lachlan immediately.

Her expression was carefully constructed into an impossibly neutral mask. "I thought you might be here."

"Do you have the chain?" he whispered, as Sorcha squeezed through the gap in the door and closed it silently behind her. She shook her head. "He has only just fallen asleep. I will do it in a few hours when he is in a deeper slumber."

"Clara –"

"I will do it, I swear," she cut in, not commenting on Lachlan slipping back into using her false name. "But for now I need to...cool off. I need to get out of here."

He grinned despite the perilous situation they were in and his ugly, unbecoming jealousy. "I know just the place, if you do not mind the company."

Sorcha knocked her hand against his in lieu of a spoken response, so Lachlan entwined their fingers and rushed her noiselessly through the palace and down a flight of steps hewn from the very bedrock itself.

"Where is everyone?" Sorcha asked in hushed tones as they descended further and further underground. The air became colder, biting at the tips of Lachlan's ears and nose.

He squeezed her hand. "Celebrating outside. They'll be at it until the early hours of the morning."

"But the coronation ceremony is tomorrow evening!"

"One day you will stop basing a faerie's lifestyle on your boring, human sensibilities," Lachlan chuckled. When they reached a blackened iron door he glanced at her. "Most of our kind aren't strong enough to get past an iron door. But, then again, most of my kind aren't princes."

Sorcha's eyes brightened in interest as she watched Lachlan blow on his hands then hold them out in front of him, inches from the door. He muttered a string of unintelligible words under his breath until the hinges creaked and the door swung open.

He swept a hand forward and gave Sorcha a mocking bow. "After you, my lady."

Her lips quirked into the hint of a smile as she walked past him into the glimmering darkness of the room. It was only then that Lachlan realised Sorcha's hair had been tidied; a fresh wave of possessive jealousy washed over him as he imagined the kelpie's hands all over her.

Did he choose that dress for her? Did he do anything to her last night when she believed that he was me? Did he –

"Lachlan?"

Sorcha was staring at him standing there in the doorway. He shook his head. "It is nothing. Keep walking."

"I cannot see."

"Your eyes will adjust," Lachlan assured her as he closed the door behind them and led Sorcha further into the room. Pinpoints of glowing, glittering light punctuated the darkness, the result of phosphorescent mushrooms growing from the floor and ceiling surrounded by all manner of gemstones. The gentle sounds of a burn flowing over porous rock could be heard echoing all around.

Lachlan wound Sorcha across the floor with practised eyes, for it was littered with recessed pits full of silken cushions and blankets. If he had truly been the one leading up the revel outside then many beautiful, lustful Seelie would have ended up in here with him in due time.

But there was only Sorcha, and she was all Lachlan wanted. Needed.

Sorcha's mismatched eyes were like gemstones themselves as they adjusted to the low light. "What is this place, Lachlan?" she asked very quietly. "What – *ah!*"

For Lachlan wrapped his arms around Sorcha's waist, picking her up and bodily tossing the two of them into the largest pit, landing on top of innumerable gold-fringed pillows. His lips founds hers before Sorcha had an opportunity to collect her thoughts, though once she worked out what was going on she eagerly reciprocated.

Sorcha slid Lachlan's shirt from his shoulders just as his fingers made quick work of the silvered chains that held up her dress. He was desperate to remove all traces of the garment; to have every inch of Sorcha's skin belonging to him and him alone.

"When the kelpie enchanted you," he asked in an undertone, breaking away from Sorcha's mouth in order to rove his eyes up and down her body. The ethereal light in the room stained her skin first blue, then green, then sunset orange and ruby red. "What did you dream of?"

Sorcha regarded him from beneath her eyelashes; even in the darkness he noticed the blush that crossed her cheeks. She glanced away. "You," she whispered. "Of course I dreamed of you."

Desire coiled up inside Lachlan like a snake, tense and ready to strike. He kicked off his breeches and rolled Sorcha on top of him, who gasped in shock and delight. He pressed his fingertips into the curve of her thighs and let out a low, longing moan.

"It is different in real life," he said. "I told you that before. Everything is better."

Sorcha bent her head low to brush her lips against Lachlan's. "Is that simply because it is real, or is there another reason?"

"I've never thought about it all that much before," he admitted. He ran a hand through Sorcha's hair, unravelling all the beautiful handiwork the kelpie had used to keep it up. Bluebells scattered all around them; Sorcha shook her head until her hair fell wild and wavy around her shoulders. "But this is you," Lachlan continued. "This is the real you, and this is the real me. I want nothing more than to experience this night with you outside of your dreams."

Sorcha smiled. She bit Lachlan's lip the way he'd done to her the first time they kissed.

"I've been waiting for that since the very moment I met you."

CHAPTER THIRTY-TWO

Sorcha

For the second time that night Sorcha crept back into Lachlan's chambers. Murdoch lay sleeping on the bed, partially obscured by the translucent curtains. The fire was low in the hearth, so Sorcha sat on the rug beside it and stared into the smouldering coals. She was sure that, if she touched them, her skin would be just as hot as they were.

I can't believe I truly lay with Lachlan.

Sorcha hadn't wanted to leave the dark, glittering cave to return to Murdoch's side. To reality. Though the last few hours with Lachlan hadn't been the product of a dream they still very much felt like one compared to what Sorcha must now do.

She ran her fingers through her hair, finding a stray bluebell that had not yet fallen out, then padded over to an oak-and-gold wardrobe to choose something else to wear. Sorcha felt filthy in her green dress, though she knew the fabric itself was almost as clean as it had been when she'd first put it on. But it was Sorcha herself that felt dirty. Wrong. Murdoch had chosen the dress for her, and she'd let Lachlan remove it.

She wished her heart would stop beating so fast.

All I need to do is unclasp the chain from Murdoch's neck. Once I do that I am done. Lachlan and the Seelie Court will be free from any danger.

And the kelpie would be forced to retreat into Loch Lomond, never to be seen by Sorcha again. It hurt her to think of such a thing, but what else could she do? Murdoch could not be left to continue masquerading as the Prince – and, from tomorrow, King – of Faeries. If they did not take his bridle from him then there would be no way to control Murdoch whatsoever.

That didn't make Sorcha feel any better.

She ended up settling for a large, billowing shirt from the wardrobe, which was clearly Lachlan's. Sorcha removed her dress, remembering Lachlan doing the same in a flurry of fingers and kisses mere hours earlier. When it whispered to the floor she slid on Lachlan's shirt over her head, which fell to just above her knees. The sheer size of it reminded her of her father's shirt.

Sorcha's heart constricted painfully in her chest. *I hope he is alright,* she thought, realising in that moment how much she missed her parents. *I hope I will see them soon.*

Whether she did or not was entirely up to what Sorcha did next.

When she reached the bed Sorcha wanted nothing more than to run away. Instead she forced herself to sit by Murdoch's side, watching as he slept so peacefully that she almost cried. *Why are you doing this?* Sorcha thought at him. She held out a shaking hand towards the delicate silver chain around his neck, shining like diamonds in the light from the dying fire. *Why did you have to pretend to be Lachlan? Why did you doom him to be a fox? Just what, exactly, are you planning?*

All Sorcha had to do was yank the chain away from Murdoch. Once it was removed he would revert to his original form and Sorcha could flee. Murdoch would have no choice but to return to the loch from whence he came or his very being would unravel.

Sorcha's part of the job was so easy. So simple.

She couldn't do it.

Sorcha traced the line of Murdoch's collarbone with her fingertips, never quite touching the chain. Her heart fluttered in her chest as her brain desperately tried to work out an alternative plan. Something. Anything. A solution that didn't involve ruining the kelpie's life.

Murdoch's eyes flashed open.

He darted a hand out and grabbed Sorcha's wrist, squeezing it painfully as he pulled it away from his neck. She cried out in shock and tried to claw his hand away, but Murdoch wouldn't budge.

"Was this your plan all along?" he asked, tone as dark and dangerous as his eyes. "Lull me into a false sense of security and -"

"No! No, I -"

"Are you sure? Because that is what you're doing, is it not?"

"But I haven't - I didn't -"

"And why not? What is staying your hand?"

Sorcha wavered. She did not know what to say. She

looked at Murdoch's fingers crushing her wrist until, eventually, he let her go. She held her arm to her chest and rubbed where he had held it, wincing at the pain. "Why are you doing this?" she asked. "You said I would find out tomorrow. I need to know now."

Murdoch sat up, a scowl warping his handsome features. "You should understand already, Sorcha. They are as bad as your own kind."

"What do you mean?"

"They are taking over the lochs!" he exclaimed. "With every year more and more of them creep along the shore, deciding that they like the water and can trick more humans from within it. Already the moors are overrun with Unseelie and many of the lakes and shorelines in England, too. And that's not to mention the selkies they entrap with forced, binding promises simply because they can. It sickens me."

Sorcha hesitated. "You said Unseelie. What about –"

"They are all the same, in the end! Seelie, Unseelie, I do not care." Murdoch clucked his tongue in disgust. "Your precious Lachlan and his brethren scorn and hate Loch Lomond and its creatures. They fear it, because they cannot control it. You do not think they would take it over if given the opportunity? Of course they would! Call what I am doing a pre-emptive strike."

"And what is it that you're doing, exactly?"

Murdoch's eyes glittered with vicious delight. "Why, I am inciting a war."

"You..." Sorcha was speechless. Murdoch's vendetta against the Fair Folk was more than a simple whim. It had been bubbling under the surface for longer than she could possibly know, and Murdoch had been biding his time until an opportune moment arose.

Sorcha – silly, mortal Sorcha Margaret Darrow – had accidentally provided him with one.

"You want the Seelie and Unseelie to fight each other until they both perish," she murmured, certain. "That has been your plan all along."

Murdoch nodded. He ran his hands through his hair to push it out of his face, exhaling deeply as he collapsed against the pillows. He glanced at Sorcha out of the corner of his eye. "So you see, Sorcha, I am not truly the villain here. You have merely become caught in the crossfire on an ongoing, centuries-long feud. It is not your fault, so do not feel responsible for the fate of your fox."

Sorcha looked at her hands, knowing that what she was about to say was going to be shot down immediately. "Why can't you all try to compromise, instead? Can't you talk it out?"

"To what end?" Murdoch snarled, back on-edge once more. "Tell me, *Miss Darrow,* would you be willing to compromise with the slew of city folk who wish to sully your beloved land? Who want nothing more than to buy you out and force every farmer, child and lowly maiden to move away? Would you?"

"I –"

"Would you?"

"Of course not!" Sorcha wailed. She did not care that there were tears streaming down her face as she locked eyes with Murdoch. "I could never do that! But this –"

"Do not dare say this is different. It is the same. You

236

wish to protect your land, and so do I. Out of everyone, I *know* you can understand me. I am not wrong here."

Sorcha averted her eyes, at a loss for what else she could say. When she tried to stand up from the bed Murdoch pulled her back down. "Let me go!" she protested, kicking at the kelpie for all the good it would do. "How dare – let me go!" But Murdoch held her tightly against his chest no matter what she did, as if he was about to stroke her hair and kiss all her troubles away.

"I cannot do that," he murmured, genuinely apologetic despite the way his hands clung to her every curve. "You know I can't. Just stay by my side, Sorcha. Don't make this harder than it already is."

Sorcha couldn't stop crying. She had failed Lachlan, and Ailith, and their entire realm. Murdoch was right, of course; she was not responsible for them. She did not owe them anything. What happened tomorrow was beyond Sorcha's control and scope of understanding. She was only human, after all.

And yet.

"I will stay," she sobbed, before swallowing away the rest of her tears. She stopped struggling against Murdoch's tightly-muscled arms, growing limp against him.

He sighed in relief. With a smile he relaxed his hold on her. "Good," he said. "Good. You are a clever girl, Sorcha. I –"

"But you will leave me alone," she interrupted, extricating herself from his grip to roll over to the other side of the bed. "You will not touch me."

Murdoch's only response was silence. He didn't

have to say anything; Sorcha could sense his sadness, anger and longing upon the very air between them.

She wondered if he could sense hers.

CHAPTER THIRTY-THREE

Lachlan

"Are you sure about this, Lachlan?"

"No, but what other choice do we have? I do not believe any of us are strong enough to defeat a kelpie on our own."

"But if we waited –"

Lachlan threw Ailith a scathing look. "The swearing-in ceremony is today. *Now.* If the kelpie is crowned king then it does not matter if the Seelie believed him to be me when it happens. The magic in the ceremony is binding; you know this, Ailith. It has to be now."

Lachlan was wearing a heavy burgundy cloak to hide his appearance from the growing crowd. Soon he would reveal his true identity, but not yet. He had to pick the right moment. He had to know that Sorcha was safe and unharmed. He had to know that he could wrangle the kelpie's silver bridle away.

For there was no doubt that, for whatever reason, Sorcha had failed in stealing it.

Did the creature catch her in the middle of the night ripping it from his throat? Did he hurt her? He better not have hurt her. Or was Sorcha simply...unable to do it?

Lachlan did not want to dwell on what that meant.

"I am worried for Miss Sorcha," Ailith murmured, as if reading Lachlan's mind. She squeezed his hand. "She is just a human, Lachlan. She should never have been brought here – not when there is so much unrest."

Lachlan snorted. "It was not as if I brought her here! It was the –"

"You allowed her to become involved in breaking your curse," she said, disconcertingly mildly. "You should never have done that."

"I could not seek help from the Court – not when Innis and Fergus were still alive and keeping watch for me. I had to stop them before the coronation ceremony, which meant I had a fortnight to get my body back. *Fourteen days,* Ailith, with no Seelie help. What would you have had me do?"

"I..."

"Precisely. Now let us get closer. Everyone expects you to be up on the plinth, anyway."

"I do not wish to be so close to the kelpie," Ailith muttered, averting her eyes. "The beast is strong. He has to be, to have held Loch Lomond as his domain for half a millennium."

Lachlan kept his eyes on the plinth as they weaved through the clamouring, excited crowd. No traces of blood remained upon the elaborately carved wooden throne which Innis had been sitting on the day before, nor upon the floor where Fergus' head had rolled.

It was as if they'd never existed at all.

"Lachlan, you are scaring me."

He looked at Ailith, realising in the process that his mouth had curled into a savage, snarling grin. "How do you know the same kelpie has resided in the loch for five hundred years?" he asked, redirecting the subject and schooling his expression in the process.

"Are you...did you listen to none of your mother's lessons as you grew up? Or any of your teachers'?"

Lachlan could only laugh. "Why would I have done, when I could rely on your far superior memory to recall such facts for me?"

Ailith said nothing; the look she gave Lachlan spoke volumes. But they had treated each other like this for the best part of a hundred years – it was the way they worked and lived and loved each other. Lachlan doubted either of them would change any time soon.

He was about to comment on the promise of rain in the twilight sky above them when the noise of the crowd hushed in one sweeping moment, only to erupt into cheers almost immediately afterwards. Lachlan and Ailith focused all of their attention onto the plinth once more; the regally dressed figure of the false Lachlan swept into the centre, bowing gracefully to the crowd as their shouting grew louder.

"He may well be better at riling up the Court than you ever were," Ailith mused in an undertone.

Lachlan rolled his eyes. "I'd crave attention, too, if I lived at the bottom of a loch for five hundred years."

And then he spotted Sorcha as she joined the kelpie on the plinth, and Lachlan's blood ran cold. For there was no doubt from the look on her pale, troubled face that something had gone dreadfully wrong the night before. He hated to see her so obviously upset after their stolen hours together.

She should be flushed and breathless and clinging to me, not a morose, crying slave to a water horse. But at least she has not been harmed.

Even thinking such a thing reminded Lachlan of the fact that the kelpie loved Sorcha; if he'd ever doubted it then the way he looked at her now, in front of everyone – with Lachlan's own eyes, no less – was all he needed to confirm his fears. Bitterly he wondered if Sorcha had not technically *failed* to steal the creature's silver chain but instead had chosen not to.

But Lachlan shook his head at such a notion. *After what we did last night I do not think she has feelings for the kelpie the way she might have done when he was Murdoch. I should have faith in her.*

"How kind of you all to be so enthusiastic after the revel last night!" the Lachlan who was not Lachlan announced, in the unnaturally loud voice he had used before he'd slaughtered Innis and Fergus. "To have your support after everything that has happened means everything to me. Queen Evanna would have loved to see you like this."

The crowd went wild, for how could they not? The kelpie knew how to manipulate them as if they were mere simple-minded humans. Lachlan cringed to witness it.

The kelpie paced back and forth. "I have a confession to make. Yesterday I was not forthcoming about my dearly departed stepfamily's plot to overthrow me. I feel I owe you a full explanation."

Lachlan froze along with the rest of the tense, excited crowd. For here would be the answers that had evaded him ever since the kelpie took his skin. Sorcha was looking anywhere but at the kelpie; she bit her lip and scanned the crowd with desperate eyes. Looking for Lachlan.

She could not see him.

We need a distraction to get her out of here, he realised. *If Sorcha is up there when we tackle the kelpie then she could get hurt.*

When he caught Ailith's eye Lachlan saw that she had reached the same conclusion and was thinking hard about a solution. But then the false Lachlan continued his speech, so the two of them temporarily redirected their attention back him.

"I had been made to believe that my suspicions towards my Unseelie stepfamily were unfounded," the kelpie said. He stopped pacing to stand in front of the faerie throne. "I was told to be tolerant. My mother loved her new husband, after all. And he loved her, too. But that was not enough to assuage my fears, and I was correct to cling to them!"

All around Lachlan the crowd was beginning to grasp what the kelpie was insinuating. It unsettled Lachlan to no end, for everything the creature was saying were his own beliefs. *Just what is he planning?*

"And so, my good, dear Seelie Court, though it pains me to be right in such a situation I have no choice but to tell you the truth: my disappearance was a direct attack from the Unseelie king himself. He would have us under his thumb, to rule and manipulate as he sees fit. This cannot stand. I will not let it stand!"

Oh, no.

Though Lachlan had hated his stepfamily and their Unseelie blood, and had not discounted the notion that their attempt to usurp the throne was indeed part of a much bigger plan, now that he was listening to somebody else say as much with his own voice Lachlan realised what a horrific mistake it would have been for him to blame the Unseelie for what happened to him.

The kelpie was starting a war, which Lachlan knew his own Court could not hope to win.

"And nor should you!"

Lachlan stared at Ailith, for it was she who had shouted. Everyone looked at her; she squeezed Lachlan's hand before sweeping up onto the plinth to join the kelpie. The creature was looking at her, suspicion clear as day on his face. Lachlan held back a grin.

He does not know Ailith. He does not love her the way Lachlan, the Prince of Faeries, should. This is the distraction we need.

Ailith smiled angelically for the kelpie, enveloping his hands with her own. She turned to the enraptured crowd. "I, too, was duped by the bloody traitor Fergus and his father. I had been ordered to end my relationship with Lachlan, though I loved him so."

Everywhere there was outrage. Lachlan used the opportunity to close the gap between him and the plinth, readying himself to spring upon it and attack the kelpie. It was then that Sorcha, finally, spotted him, and her face paled. Lachlan frowned; he had thought Sorcha would be relieved to see him.

The kelpie seemed at a loss for what to do in the

face of Ailith's physical proximity. "We were all duped," he said. "We –"

"And I love you still!" Ailith cried, before embracing the false Lachlan, running a hand across his face and kissing him.

Now is your chance, Ailith, Lachlan thought. *Grab the chain and I'll grab Sorcha.*

The crowd was going wild at the kiss, eyes blind to the glassiness of their prince's expression. But their delight turned to shock when 'Lachlan' wrenched Ailith away and tossed her to the floor, a look of unbridled disgust upon his face.

"You –"

"How dare you lay a hand on her," Lachlan raged, throwing away his cloak as he jumped up onto the plinth. All around were gasps and exclamations of shock, and then –

Silence.

The kelpie stared at Lachlan in wide-eyed disbelief. "You should be a fox."

"And you should be in the loch, where you belong, yet here you are. So let Sorcha go and leave this place."

Lachlan watched as the kelpie dropped his disguise, returning to Murdoch Buchanan's appearance. The very air seemed to crackle around him; he ignored Lachlan to stare at Sorcha with fathomless, empty eyes.

"No."

CHAPTER THIRTY-FOUR

Sorcha

For one excruciatingly long moment nothing but silence surrounded Sorcha. She did not know who to look at: Lachlan, whose face was coloured with anger and concern at the way Murdoch had tossed Ailith to the floor; Ailith, who looked grimly satisfied that she had shown the crowd who the Lachlan preparing to take the crown actually was; the crowd, who did not yet truly understand what was going on, or Murdoch.

Murdoch, who had dropped his disguise and was staring right at Sorcha as if nobody else existed.

"No," he said, and though his voice was quiet it carried across the entire clearing. "You cannot have her. And you cannot have your kingdom, either."

The air around Murdoch seemed almost liquid. It ebbed and flowed around him, distorting the trees and flowers and sky. And the strange effect was spreading; when it reached the crowd the faeries in the front line froze in place, jaws gone slack as their eyes lost all life.

Wordlessly they pushed through the throng to reach the burn which encircled the clearing. They knelt in front of it. Nobody spoke.

Then they dunked their heads into the deepest part of the water and everyone screamed.

"Somebody pull them out of the burn!" Ailith cried, getting to her feet as she spoke. "They are drowning!"

But more and more Seelies joined them in their suicidal enchantment instead, until the water was brimming with thrashing, oxygen-starved bodies. Lachlan took a step towards Murdoch, face contorted with fury, but the kelpie held a hand out to stop him.

"Come any closer and I'll drown your beloved Ailith next," he warned. "How dare you pursue Miss Darrow when you had her, fox. How *dare* you."

Lachlan could only shake his head in disbelief. "Your problem is with me, not my people. Stop what you are doing!"

"Are you truly so arrogant as to assume this is all because of a grudge against *you*?" Murdoch laughed; it was an ugly, twisted sound. "Seelie, Unseelie – you are all the same. Self-centred, vain, arrogant creatures who covet anything they do not have, and scheme and bribe and blackmail until they possess it!"

"A war will destroy us all!"

"Exactly."

Lachlan's chest was heaving as he swung his head around, taking in the sight of the kelpie's ongoing massacre. "You will not get away with this," he said, but Murdoch merely snorted at the useless exclamation.

"Anyone who was here today to witness this will *die*

today. They will die, and I will blame it on the Unseelie, and I shall remain as you – as king – until you are all destroyed."

Sorcha had to do something. She knew it, so why was she standing there merely watching as dozens upon dozens of faeries slowly drowned themselves? Ailith was rushing around trying desperately to pull those closest to her out of the burn alongside a handful of Seelie Court guards who were still unaffected by the kelpie's strange, murderous powers. Sorcha was likewise unaffected; she could help them.

But when she moved forward to do so it was Lachlan, not Murdoch, who rushed towards her and pulled her away. His golden eyes bored into her own. "Get out of here, you fool!" he demanded. "Run away whilst you still can. *Please.*"

"Sorcha will not leave me," Murdoch called over, certain. He smiled at her, so agonisingly innocent in his surety that she would do as he said that Sorcha had to dig her nails into her palms to keep herself from crying. For even after she had told him not to touch her in the dead of night – to leave her alone to shake and shiver herself to sleep – the kelpie clearly had no doubt that he could make things right between them once today was over.

But he couldn't. Sorcha could not allow him to murder hundreds of members of the Seelie Court in front of her very eyes.

"Stand aside, Lachlan," she said in an undertone. His eyes widened when he saw her expression, but then, slowly, he nodded in understanding and let Sorcha past him. She walked towards the kelpie, careful to keep her face calm and collected. When she reached the dark-haired man she saw his eyes were wild and blood-thirsty; Sorcha knew nothing she said to him would make him stop.

Except, perhaps, one very specific, lone word.

"Murdoch," she murmured, stroking the kelpie's cheek with the tips of her fingers. His face lost some of its madness for just a moment, and all around them the sound of a hundred faeries breaking through water to claw and gasp at air filled Sorcha's ears.

Murdoch's lips curled into just the hint of a smile. "You have never used his first name before. Not to me. I rather like it, Sorcha. I –"

Her hand moved to his neck and snapped his silver chain.

"You should have kept me enchanted until you were crowned king," Sorcha said through tears, for in front of her it was clear the kelpie's heart was breaking. "Why didn't you simply keep me enchanted? Why allow me to be myself?"

Murdoch swallowed. It was his own form that was shimmering now, not the air. He closed his eyes for a moment. "I sent Galileo back to your parents' house, Miss Darrow. He is fond of you. Please look after him for me."

"You did not answer me!" Sorcha yelled, reaching up on her tiptoes to run a hand through Murdoch's hair to try and force his face down to her level. "If your plan was so important to you then why –"

"You already know why." Murdoch's voice was so quiet nobody but Sorcha could hear his confession. "I think everybody knows, even your fox. I am sorry I did not meet you in person sooner. Before him. Perhaps I

249

should have remained your Mr Buchanan and never come to this wicked place at all."

"Mur-"

When Murdoch finally bent his head towards hers Sorcha thought he was going to kiss her. But then the lines of his body warped and disappeared and, in the space of three wretched seconds, he became the kelpie once more.

The huge, monstrous stallion reared onto his hind legs and screamed, his dark eyes tragically sad and betrayed. Sorcha could only watch him, clinging uselessly to the broken silver chain, as he leapt from the plinth in a flurry of shattered wood and crying, panicked faeries rolling out of his way.

"Return from whence you came, kelpie!" Lachlan yelled above all the deathly commotion. The creature turned to face him, baring his unnaturally sharp teeth in response. But he could not attack; his powers had been stripped from him along with his bridle. "Fall into the deepest, darkest depths of the loch and do not let any of my kind see you again, for if we do then know that your bridle will be melted down to nothing."

Sorcha wanted the kelpie to look at her just as badly as she dearly hoped he wouldn't. But he turned tail and fled through the forest without doing so, leaving Sorcha looking at the chain in her hands, instead. It had returned to its original form, allowing her to see – for the first time – the intricate links and loops and lengths of metal and blackened leather that constructed it.

"You did it, Sorcha. You truly did it."

Sorcha did not hear Lachlan at first; it was only when he picked her up and spun her around that her brain understood what he had said. She forced a smile upon her face for the obviously delighted faerie. "I said I would, did I not?"

Lachlan seemed barely aware of the pandemonium all around him when he kissed Sorcha. She wrapped her arms around his neck, clinging to him as if his presence might somehow keep her grounded.

"Miss Sorcha?"

Lachlan turned Sorcha around with him to face Ailith, who curtsied to them both. She was drenched from her efforts to save her people; behind them Sorcha couldn't help but notice the dozen or so twisted bodies of faeries lying in the burn who would never move again.

A chill ran down her spine.

"We owe you a debt of gratitude," the beautiful faerie said. "You must stay and live as one of us so we can repay you."

Lachlan's eyes lit up at the suggestion. He placed Sorcha back on her feet, took a step back from her and dropped down into a low, sweeping bow. "It would be our privilege and honour to have one as brave as you within our number."

But Sorcha shook her head. She had never wanted immortality, nor to live within the Seelie Court for the rest of her life. The way she felt for Lachlan was not enough to change that. She knew that he knew that, despite what he was currently asking. "You know I do not want that, Lachlan – Ailith – though it is beyond generous," she said, smiling sadly. "You may believe me a fool for refusing such an offer, but I..."

"I understand," Lachlan replied, though his expression was glum and disheartened. "Perhaps, in time, I might convince you otherwise."

"Perhaps," she said, for there was no harm in allowing the faerie a small shred of hope. "Perhaps one day, if my parents ever try to force me to marry a Londoner again."

It was a joke, but Lachlan did not laugh. He held out a hand towards Sorcha. "The bridle," he said. "We will protect it."

"*No!*"

Sorcha hadn't meant to react so viscerally. She clutched Murdoch's bridle protectively to her chest, though the hurt in both Lachlan and Ailith's eyes was plain to see. She sighed. "No," she said again, gentler this time. "I wish to keep it. I was the one who took it; it is mine."

Lachlan said nothing. Sorcha knew that, by his kind's own laws, he could not take the bridle from her. It *was* Sorcha's. He ran a hand through his hair and averted his eyes, clearly at a loss for what to say or do. Eventually he asked, "You are returning home now, aren't you? You really will not stay?"

"My father is sick," Sorcha explained, making her way off the plinth and towards the long pathway home as she did so. Part of her instinctively knew that if she stayed within the faerie realm for a final night then she may not leave at all. "I must go home. I cannot delay any further; it is high time I acted like the adult I am and faced my responsibilities head-on."

He chuckled. "I would prefer that you didn't. But I can see you again? When will I see you again?"

Sorcha turned to look at Lachlan over her shoulder, flashing him a grin that was clearly too infectious for him not to reciprocate, though they both knew her smile was tinged with a sadness Sorcha might never recover from.

"You know where I like to sing."

EPILØGUE

Sorcha

September rolled into October before Sorcha was truly aware of it and, with it, she turned twenty years old.

She never imagined she'd be forbidden to leave the Darrow grounds at *twenty years old.*

Sorcha supposed she couldn't blame her parents for keeping her locked up. She'd run away, after all. When she'd returned without Murdoch Buchanan only to discover that Galileo was indeed tied up in her father's stable Sorcha had to come up with a plausible excuse for why the man had disappeared, but his horse had not.

Even now, weeks later, she was sure her parents did not believe that Murdoch simply returned to London on urgent business, leaving behind his beloved stallion because Sorcha had grown fond of it. But – perhaps because they hoped it meant their daughter may still marry the man – neither her mother nor father questioned her lie. And Sorcha *was* fond of Galileo. Her parents only allowed her to leave the house at all because of him; to care for him.

Sorcha would ride him down to the loch shore simply to stare at the grey, wintry water. It almost looked to be made of steel. She hadn't dared touch the loch, fearing that the kelpie would sense her presence and drag her down into the depths to join him.

Sorcha was equally terrified that he *wouldn't.*

That the kelpie would ignore her, and Sorcha would never see or feel him again in the water, constricted the muscles of her heart until she could hardly breathe. Sorcha always fled back to the Darrow house on Galileo the moment she felt this way. She didn't *want* to feel this way, but neither did she wish to forget about the kelpie.

Because she'd been locked inside the house Sorcha had not been to her favourite spot to sing even once. She was therefore yet to see Lachlan; he hadn't even crept into her dreams.

He must be busy, she reasoned late one night, tossing and turning restlessly as sleep – not for the first time – evaded her. *He is king now, after all. I am not important.*

Thinking as much caused Sorcha's heart to tighten just as it did when dwelling on the kelpie. It wasn't that she revelled in being special or important to either of them – it was that they'd grown very much important to *her.* And she missed Lachan greatly. Sorcha wanted nothing more than to see him, for she did not want their short, tumultuous time together to become a faded memory as years passed by, and she grew older, and he did not. She wanted more. She wasn't done; her relationship with the faerie felt as if it had barely started.

Just as Sorcha closed her eyes and decided that she

should genuinely try and get some sleep she heard a rapping on her window. She stilled, listening patiently as the wooden frame was pried open from the outside. A horrifically bitter gust of wind whistled into her room; she ducked her head beneath the covers and tightened them around her.

But Sorcha was not worried about who the intruder was, for there was only one person who would do such a thing in the middle of the night, and she had only just been thinking of said person.

Or, rather, faerie.

"You have not been in your usual place, Clara."

Sorcha smiled at the sound of the familiar voice, though she did not open her eyes. "You won't call me by my real name, King Lachlan of the Seelie Court?"

"I decided I like Clara too much to abandon it. It is the name you gave me to use, so it is mine. Where have you been over the past few weeks?"

"Under house arrest. I was sorry to miss your coronation."

When Sorcha heard the window shut she finally turned over to face it, then lowered the covers from her head and opened her eyes. Lachlan was perched on the sill, a lopsided grin twisting his lips. The moonlight shone behind him. It illuminated his hair and skin alike with brilliant white-gold; a wicked glint set his molten eyes on fire.

"I almost came to steal you away for it, you know," he said before climbing down onto her bed. Sorcha moved over to make room for him, so Lachlan eagerly slid beneath the covers and propped his head up on his hand to stare at her.

Sorcha was glad for the darkness in her room to hide the blush that spread across her cheeks. "Why didn't you come for me, then?"

"If you'd wanted to go to the coronation you would have made it known. I thought the best thing I could do was wait for you to appear in the forest, looking for me."

"Considering your presence in my bed at present I somehow doubt that."

Lachlan held a hand over his mouth to cover a snicker. Sorcha was glad for it; her father would likely have a heart attack if he opened the door to find a faerie in his daughter's room.

"I grew impatient, admittedly," Lachlan said. "Do you wish for me to go?"

Sorcha shook her head. She glanced out of the window just as a blast of wind buffeted against the pane – the mere sound of it screamed *cold* and *unpleasant* at her. She raised herself up on her elbows, tilting her head towards Lachlan's. "It sounds awful out there."

"It *is* awful. My journey here was rather rough."

"You must be weary. Would you care to spend the night here, King of Faeries?"

Lachlan whispered a hand along Sorcha's thigh, smiling with his brilliantly white teeth at her resultant intake of breath. He leaned his head forward and bit her lip. "I shall gladly take you up on such a generous offer, Clara."

Sorcha had always hated the anglicisation of her name. Now she adored it. *Only when he says it,* she thought, slinging her arms around Lachlan's neck to pull him on top of her. *Only for him. Nobody else.*

In the morning Sorcha could worry about her parents, and taking over her father's responsibilities, and what was going to happen when more English investors showed up vying to buy their land. She could continue to stare at the loch and mull over the kelpie, and wonder if it might simply be better to run off to the Seelie Court and live with the faeries forever.

But, at least for now, Sorcha did not have to dwell over the unknowable concept of forever. Lachlan was with her, and they wanted each other, and 'now' only lasted a night.

Everything else could wait until tomorrow.

THE STORY CONTINUES IN LORD OF HORSES...

Murdoch

Murdoch loved the water more than anything, and he loved the water of the loch he lived in most of all.

Spending two years banished to the bottom of it by the golden faerie king and his ice-blue queen changed his perspective on things.

In truth Murdoch wasn't even Murdoch. He'd taken the unfortunate Mister Buchanan's name, as well as his face and memories, when he'd dragged the man down into the loch and consumed his body and soul. But Murdoch didn't have the guise of the human anymore; without his bridle he could not change his form at all.

He liked the man's name, though, so even now he kept it.

For months Murdoch mulled and glowered and rued his fate at the very bottom of Loch Lomond. There was nothing else he could do, after all. If he dared show up at the surface and was spied by a damned faerie then his bridle would be destroyed, and Murdoch would have no chance of ever recovering his full powers again.

He'd had no intention of risking his very existence by leaving the depths of the loch. He truly hadn't. That was, until Murdoch heard something that changed his priorities entirely.

For there were plans to fill in the shallow, southern shores of his home, funded by the very company Murdoch Buchanan himself had worked for, before the kelpie had devoured him. He had to do something to stop the plan. If he didn't then Murdoch would not be the only one who suffered.

He desperately needed to talk to Sorcha Darrow.

Out now!

Read on for an excerpt from *Intended:*

H. L. Macfarlane's brand new mythology-soaked fantasy!

• • •

A long silence stretched out, then, save for the twittering of a handful of morning birds which remained in Mt. Duega for the winter. Charlie tuned into the sound, breathing in the crisp air in an effort to reassure herself that she was not all that far from home – not really. She was still surrounded by her beloved woods. It *sounded* like her woods. It *smelled* like her woods.

Daniel Silver was staring straight at her.

Charlie flinched, then hated herself for doing so. The last thing she needed was for the man to think she was intimidated by him, though in truth she was. So when he beckoned with a finger for her to come closer Charlie bit back her nerves and walked towards him.

I feel like he's trying to work me out in one fell swoop, she mused, when Silver's gaze swept from her feet to her head, back down again, then settled on her eyes. For a moment Charlie genuinely believed that he *could* get her measure so quickly, and pushed out her Influence on instinct in order to direct him elsewhere.

But before the tendril of magic could reach Silver, Charlie coiled it back in. Her father would hate it if she Influenced her new employer – and she agreed with him. *It will only make my life harder,* she concluded. *I'd have to keep my magic active at all times to stop him from realising someone is working it upon him in the first place.*

For Charlie had no doubts left in her mind about just how powerful Daniel Silver was now that she was finally in close proximity to him. Her father hadn't lied; the raw magic emanating off him was staggering. The urge to Influence him returned, just for a moment, when Charlie's curiosity over how much of her own magic she'd have to use to break through Silver's defences overwhelmed her.

Once more Charlie had to reign herself in. *Focus on something else. Like his glasses. They're definitely prescription,* she thought, tilting her head to see the slight distortion the lenses caused to Silver's face.

"Just what is it that you're thinking, Miss Hope?" the man asked, noting where Charlie's attention was with passive interest.

"That a magician as strong as you shouldn't be

wearing glasses."

"Coming from a young woman who didn't deem it necessary to brush her hair nor tuck in her shirt for her first day at a new job?"

Both quips left their respective tongues in close succession of each other, leaving Charlie in no doubt what the man's first impression of her was. *So he's obsessed with image,* she concluded, glancing down to see that her shirt was indeed untucked. She made no attempt to fix it nor to tidy her hair, which was always unkempt when Charlie left it unbound.

Her decision not to tidy herself up was clearly noted by Silver. His nose wrinkled in distaste, causing his glasses to slide downwards. When he pushed then back up Charlie couldn't help but say, "That wouldn't happen if you fixed your eyesight."

"My personal preferences aren't of your concern. Are you always this rude upon meeting people for the first time?"

"Rude?" Charlie blinked her eyes innocently. "I'm merely making an observation."

"Yes, with the intent of being rude."

Oh, you have no idea, she thought, resisting the urge to say something else that would most definitely be construed as such. Instead, Charlie crossed her arms over her chest and attempted to stare down her new employer. When he remained silent she asked, "So where am I staying, anyway? Or are we going to stand out here all day?"

In lieu of answering her question Silver took a

step towards her and mirrored Charlie's crossed arms. Another frown furrowed his brow, causing his glasses to slip once more.

Behind the lenses Charlie noted his eyes were very, very blue.

"Are you a Mind or Matter magician?" Silver demanded, clearly discomfited by the fact he hadn't been able to work it out yet.

Charlie resisted the urge to smile at this invisible victory, then replied honestly, "I'm useless with Matter."

"Mind, then. Any specific strengths?"

"I don't know. I guess you'll have to find out for your-"

"Miss Hope, I'm warning you. I don't have the patience to deal with this attitude of yours."

"I guess you'll have to fire me, then."

For the briefest of moments Charlie was certain that Silver was about to explode. His temple twitched, and his hands gripped his forearms with tense, barely-constrained irritation. She prepared herself for a shout. A curse. An immediate dismissal.

Instead Silver closed his eyes, exhaled, then turned back towards his expansive house. "Uthesh give me strength, I understand exactly what you're doing. Follow me, Miss Hope."

Well that didn't work out the way I wanted it to, Charlie sulked, nonetheless dutifully following Mr Silver into his abode. *I suppose Da would never forgive me if I deliberately got myself fired.*

The man strode far too quickly through his house for Charlie to make out much of her surroundings, but since the morning sunlight hadn't reached the corridors yet she knew it was pointless to try and memorise the layout, anyway. When a tawny cat leapt from a shadowy windowsill into Silver's arms moments later Charlie jumped in fright.

But then Mr Silver smiled, and all she could focus on was him.

Gone was his detached demeanour and barely-contained temper. Faint lines creased the sides of his eyes, which lit up at the mere sight of the animal. He looked happy. Normal.

Like a mortal human being, not a man who was going to live forever.

"Kit," Silver said to the cat, scratching its chin before bopping its forehead with his own. "Just where have you been hiding all these weeks?"

The cat – Kit – mewed in response before turning its impossibly green eyes on Charlie. She took a small step back in shock.

It's from the woods. Daniel Silver is friends with an animal kin of the Immortal Folk?

Charlie supposed she shouldn't be surprised. Silver's estate was right on the boundary of Duega woods and he was immortal himself. It *shouldn't* have been a surprise.

Except that it was.

Never in all her twenty-four years had Charlie known another soul who fraternised with creatures from the woods.

When Kit meowed at her Charlie was brought starkly back into the present. Silver was staring at her staring at his cat, who jumped from his arms to slink down the corridor. Charlie turned her head to watch Kit leave until he disappeared around a corner.

"Miss Hope."

"Yes?" she murmured, attention still on the tawny forest cat.

"In here," Silver said, opening a door on his left and indicating inside when Charlie finally focused on him once more. All signs of his previous easy smile were gone.

Numbly Charlie entered the room, careful to give Mr Silver a wide berth as she did so. Her Influence magic was exacerbated by close contact; for years now she had barely touched another soul, save her father.

Inside the room was sparsely furnished with high-quality, oak-carved pieces: a high-backed bed, a wardrobe, a chest of drawers, a desk, a full-length mirror and a chair.

"My Chief-of-Staff will deal with you shortly," Silver said when Charlie perched upon the bed, testing the spring of the mattress with splayed fingers. "Don't treat her with the same disrespect you have thus far shown me."

Charlie clucked her tongue, keeping her eyes averted as she muttered, "I wouldn't dream of it."

The shudder of the door not-quite-slamming

closed was all the reply Charlie got. But when she strained her ears she just barely heard Silver lament, "Just what have I agreed to?"

She threw herself onto her back with a smile. Silver may have worked out that she was trying to get fired but that didn't mean he *wouldn't* fire her.

After all, if Charlie was the most incompetent employee Daniel Silver had ever taken on then he'd have no choice but to dismiss her...or risk the wrath of his political sponsors who had all so desperately wished to have their children taken under the man's wing.

A small, mischievous laugh left Charlie's lips. "I give him a week."

• • •

H. L. Macfarlane's *Intended* is an enchanting adult fairy tale ideal for fans of Uprooted, Howl's Moving Castle, and Shadow & Bone.

ACKNOWLEDGEMENTS

To have finally written a Scots-inspired faerie tale makes me very happy. I was completely engrossed in the research and writing of Prince of Foxes, and I can't wait to write the sequels, either.

Though the Foxes trilogy is technically set within the Chronicles of Curses universe it feels a little different to the three books that have preceded it, and the ones that will follow in that series. Why, you ask? Because it's steeped in lots of Scottish and British history! I think it makes Prince of Foxes feel altogether more realistic, though I may be wrong. I suppose that's up to you to decide! Either way, that's why I separated Foxes and its sequels into a new trilogy.

At first Murdoch was just going to be an outright villain, but – shock horror – I completely fell in love with him and decided he deserved better. Ironically that makes his fate at the end of this book even more tragic. Oh well; torturing characters is one of my favourite things to do. And things are not over for him, anyway!

I can't wait for you to read what's next. Until next time!

ORIGIN OF POEMS

Fox Sleep (W. S. Merwin; 1992)
A Vision (Robert Burns; 1794)
O Can Ye Sew Cushions (Robert Burns; 1787)
Home (Robert Burns; 1786)

ABOUT THE AUTHOR

Hayley Louise Macfarlane hails from the very tiny hamlet of Balmaha on the shores of Loch Lomond in Scotland. After graduating with a PhD in molecular genetics she did a complete 180 and moved into writing fiction. Though she loves writing multiple genres (fantasy, romance, sci-fi, psychological fiction and horror so far!) she is most widely known for her Gothic, Scottish fairy tale, Prince of Foxes – book one of the Bright Spear trilogy.

Printed in Great Britain
by Amazon

73019488R00166